Spiritual Siege

Alex raised her head, her gray eyes glowing with sparks of indescribable color.

"You will give us the sworn one. He is ours. He will go with us and all will be as it was." The voice was sweet, reasonable, coaxing their hearts.

Derek said firmly, "I cannot allow that."

The wind hit the windows all at once, rattling the frames.

"If you're going to attack, get it over with," he said to the room at large. "Enough with the talking! Take him, or leave us be!"

At his words, Alex's body shook like a marionette with tangled strings, her mouth opened, and a new voice came through. It cut through the warmth of the library like a serrated blade.

"Why do you interfere? By what right? Has he sworn to you as well?"

"No," Derek was forced to admit. "He has not. But he has asked us for aid and protection. To us, that is a tie as binding as any oath."

The voice speaking within Alex hesitated, searching for the right word. It found one.

"Tough."

And Alex collapsed on the floor.

For Peter,
who understood "in sickness and in health,"
but had to learn about
"in manuscript and in page proof."

And in loving memory of
Gertrude Bick Shapiro.
Miss ya, grandma.

Thanks due, and happily given, to:

Josepha Sherman, who never flinched,
no matter how odd the question—or how early;
Keith DeCandido, because *It's All His Fault*;
Katherine Lawrence, for taking the time;
Jennifer Heddle, for not even *threatening* to quit;
and #jygml, who were my late-night lifeline to
(in)sanity.
Lunatics, all of you.

And, of course,
the cast and crew of *Poltergeist: The Legacy*.™
Thanks for giving me such wonderful characters
and settings to play with!

*Since the beginning of time,
Mankind has existed between
the
World of Light and the World
of Darkness.*

*Our secret society has been
here forever.
Protecting others from the
creatures who inhabit
the shadows and the night,*

*known only to the initiated by
our true name . . .*

The Legacy

But for light to exist, darkness
must also exist.
And what falls in the shadows
between is not always evil,
but sometimes only lost . . .

PROLOGUE

He was in woods he didn't recognize; unmannered, unkept, unhealthy woods, with harsh bare branches that tore at his clothing and tangled in his hair and ground underfoot slick with a carpet of wet rocks and mud. He kept his head low, arms close to his sides as he ran, to present the smallest target.

Please, no. Please. Let me ... just let me ... don't fall ...

His breathing was harsh in his ears, the damp air causing a tickling in the back of his throat and the mold spores in the air making him want to sneeze. A pale, opalescent fog swirled around him, cat-footed tendrils that poked and pawed and made it difficult to see. He batted it away, his eyes rolling like a spooked horse, but it curled back onto him like something alive with sentience and intent.

Sweat ran down the line of his spine, pooling at the base of his back where the waistband of doeskin pants rode. Finely tanned and stitched, they would have been worth a fortune in any trendy boutique. His shirt, a light silken material, had been brightly colored once. Now, both shirt and pants were coated with mud and slicked with rain, an ugly, splotched brown. Rips in the sleeves and abraded leather at the knee showed evidence of his haste, as did the twigs and leaves caught in his hair. Normally a sleek fall of black that touched his shoulders, it was a rat's nest of tangles now, as muddied as his clothing.

Thick sweat dripped off his forehead, mixing with the mist and worsening the streaks of dirt on his face. His expression was that of a creature moved beyond fear. Beyond pain. Beyond everything save the overwhelming instinct to escape.

But like the doe which had first worn the leather of his pants, the hunters on his heels were keen and fierce, and they never ever ever gave up.

Jumping over a fallen log that appeared suddenly in his path as though hewn by malicious sprites, he landed on a particularly wet spot. Slipping and windmilling his arms wildly in order to maintain his balance, he teetered for a second before recovering in a half-crouch.

No! Steady, don't screw this up, you idiot . . .

Not taking the time to steady himself further he plowed on, sliding sideways through a patch of brush that clawed at him with small, sharp brambles.

Something scurried in the underbrush off to his left, and he flinched away from it. He heard the mocking laugh of a crow above, and it sent a shudder ripping through his body out of proportion to the sound.

Shaking off the fear, he plunged through the trees again, pushing off against a rough-barked tree.

His well-worn boots slapped against the now-rocky ground, and he gasped once, tripping over a tangle of roots. Falling to his hands and knees, he looked back as though to reassure himself that the roots had stayed put and had not risen up to entangle themselves around his ankles or pull him tighter to the ground.

The mist caught up with him as he crouched there, fouling his throat and nostrils with moisture that did nothing to sooth his inflamed nasal passages.

Thus goaded, he pushed back to his feet, running again, a sound that might have been a whimper escaping from between numbed lips. There was a path ahead, but he distrusted it, distrusted anything that looked easy. Anything that looked inviting. They were cruel, the ones chasing him, and traps were their favorite form of play.

Three steps, four. Lungs burning, legs trembling. He couldn't go on much farther.

There was a faint noise behind him, something that might have been the baying of hounds, or the clop-clip of horses' hooves, or the muted scream of a valkyrie in full flight. He checked his forward rush as it echoed endlessly, frozen like a deer at the sound of a hunter's horn.

No. Please, no . . .

His face turned up as though scouting his next direction, and eyes the blue of a summer's sky shone briefly in the late afternoon dimness before flickering back down to watch out for rocks under his traveling feet. He mumbled something incoherent that might have been a prayer or a curse. His voice, even in whisper, was raw; his throat damaged.

The sound came again from behind him, like the mocking call of a crow, the cough of a crouching tiger. They were closer. Much closer. His frantic gaze darted left, then right, seeing nothing but rocks, bramble, and stunted, withered trees. Escape was impossible. Defense, impossible. He should just turn and face them, bow his head and let the punishment begin.

No! Something human flickered in his eyes, a flash of pride, of determination. He could not accept failure now.

3

He had come this far. Come so far, all on his own. To give in now, to die now, would be letting them win. And he had sworn never to let them win.

They thought they had him. They thought he would be a good little rabbit and fall over in fright of their anger. But he wasn't alone. He had made it this far, and now his allies waited. He could feel it, taste it past the blood that pooled in his mouth and nose. It had been singing him in, a mother's touch, a father's strong arms. Human and secure. Someplace that drew him on forward like a homing beacon, pulling him through this unfamiliar place at speed that was almost guaranteed to break his neck. If he could only make it there and claim sanctuary. He knew the stories now. Knew if he could only grab hold, and hold on, he would be safe . . .

Behind him the hunters gathered for the kill; but ahead, somewhere, was hope.

The foliage cleared slightly, more rocks than brush as he continued to run downhill, following his instinct. He jumped up onto a large rock, almost a boulder, as though getting out of the mud would be enough to keep them from tracking him, and risked a glance upward. The sky was overcast, heavy with gray clouds that promised even more rain. No sunlight. He would have willingly died if he could have just felt the warmth of sunlight on his face one more time . . .

A sound, the snapping of branches behind him, and he bolted once again, calling a new burst of speed from somewhere deep within his battered and abused body. His vision blurred by sweat and tears, his nose bleeding and his lungs bursting, he managed one last heave of his body and came to a small rock-strewn bluff overlooking a turbulent gray sea.

And there, in the distance, he could see the outline of the refuge that had been calling to him, calling and coaxing and promising safety. It seemed to glow in the twilight, reflecting in the water separating them like some unholy joke.

A sobbing laugh burned in his raw throat. Water. Running water, of a sort. If he could get to the water, he would be safe. It would stop them—in their current form, at least. For a while.

And by then . . . at worse, he would drown. Not such a bad fate, compared to what awaited him should he fall.

Ignoring the screaming sinews which demanded that he collapse then and there, he stumbled forward once again. Dropping to his hands and knees, he swung his body over the side of the bluff, feeling sand and dirt intermingled give way under his weight. His legs kicked out, windmilling wildly, and he risked a glance downward to find purchase for his feet. Instead, his gaze focused on the narrow strip of rocky beach below. Almost twenty feet below.

"God, help me," he whispered, more a demand than a prayer.

And then he let go.

He hit the beach with a hollow thud, feeling the impact as just another insult to his injured body. Unable to stand, he dragged himself forward into the cold, unfriendly waters just as a wave rolled up and slapped him in the face. The temperature was a shock unlike any he could remember, and he laughed, a frightening scraped-raw croak, with the sheer pain of it.

Pain made you know you were alive. Pain let you know you were free.

Splashing down like a creature twice his slender mass, he lifted his arms, kicked out once with his legs, and began to swim for the far-off island and its promise of sanctuary.

Behind him, at the treeline, a host of shadows came out into the evening air. Hunters, gathered for an afternoon of sport. Their clothing brightly-colored, their horses gaily caparisoned and impossible under those conditions, they seemed insubstantial, like phantoms. But phantoms that exuded menace and a seething, roiling anger. All directed at the lone figure, even now stroking his way deeper into the water and away from their grasp.

For now.

But he would not escape.

ONE

M embers of the organization known only as the Legacy swore an oath when they joined that they would stand forever between humanity and the evil that constantly threatened it. However, on a calm, sunny afternoon in September, the only threat the members of the San Francisco chapter house were fighting off was boredom.

Tucked in a small, well-lit room in a corner of the great stone mansion that housed them, Derek Rayne frowned at the ancient text in front of him, occasionally turning its pages with hands encased in thin latex gloves. The odds were high that this was nothing more than it seemed, a beautifully inked and colored text on the properties of certain herbal remedies. But the circumstances of how it came into the Legacy's possession mandated care and caution.

After all, something about this book had caused the monks in the abbey where it was illuminated to place it under secure guard for hundreds of years, with not even the Holy See knowing it was hidden away. And once uncovered . . . Once uncovered, something in these pages had last month caused the death of the priest who first attempted to study it, in a manner Derek wouldn't wish on anyone.

Allegedly caused, the Prefect of the Legacy House reminded himself. Allegedly. Don't jump ahead of the known facts just yet. There was nothing to connect this manuscript to that death save circumstantial evidence of it having been what the scholar had been working on at the moment of his death.

And the manuscript itself gave off such a feeling of peace, of calm introspection, that it was difficult, if not impossible, to believe that it could be involved in bloodshed, even as an inert witness.

Not that they hadn't been fooled before, he acknowledged. By objects, and by people, all hiding their malign intent behind ordinary faces. Too often the most mundane artifice could hide terrible evil. Hence his precautions, even though his instincts were telling him that there was nothing threatening here.

But sometimes, care and caution won't get the job done properly. And if there was one thing in the mortal world that Derek Rayne hated with a passion, it was failing to decipher a mystery. He took it rather personally.

His full lips tightened for an instant, then relaxed into a faint, ironic smile that barely tugged the corners upwards against gravity. There were times when his overwhelming need to discover the truth, to *know*, translated into unbearable arrogance. Or so he had been told. Repeatedly, and at great length, by great many people.

Some of them had meant it kindly. More hadn't.

With doctorates in both Biological Anthropology and Theology, Derek Rayne knew that he made many people uneasy. That, coupled with his more unusual—and un-predictable—psi abilities, were enough to label him an outcast from much of society. But within the select circle of those who knew of the Legacy's existence, who fought the Darkness, the forty-something-year-old scientist was held in extreme high esteem.

Of course, that never stopped those people—his own team among them—from taking him down a peg or two as they felt it was needed. If pride goeth before a fall, Derek thought, he had many little helpers out to make sure his path was clear.

Shaking off those distracting thoughts, he applied himself once again to the manuscript, his eyes narrowing in concentration. It was no use: the mental vibrations were keeping him from being impartial.

Slowly, he stripped off one glove, wanting to feel the texture of the preserved paper under his skin, as though that tactile clue would give him the answers he needed to solve this perplexing question once and for all.

A noise distracted him, and he looked up, hand poised over the page, to see a young, attractive Black woman standing in the doorway. He smiled in greeting, a full, honest smile this time. "Alex. I thought you were going to go into town this afternoon."

She didn't return his smile, and only then did Derek notice that Alex had knocked on the wooden door frame to get his attention rather than to breeze in as she usually did. And once he looked up, she still remained there, watching him with those wise, dark eyes. The distance she maintained suggested that she—the only other member of the Legacy with psychic gifts like his own—had the same mixed feelings about the manuscript that he did. Interesting.

"What is it?" His accent, a low French Canadian tenor, thickened slightly, as it always did when he found himself faced with a potential problem. And that look on her face, that hesitation, indicated a problem. But of what magnitude? he wondered.

"Alex?"

"We've got a visitor," the young woman informed him, still leaning against the door frame, watching him watch her. Alexandra Moreau had a certain aura about her, a legacy from her Creole grandmother perhaps, that often made even the most commonplace of statements seem more exotic, more evocative. Or perhaps his senses open to the nuances of the manuscript, he was picking up something she wasn't even aware of yet.

Or perhaps he was merely tired and overreacting.

Derek frowned. "We weren't expecting anyone. Were we? Who is it?"

"We're not quite sure," she replied, her dark eyes still worried, but the expression on her lovely face deadpan, as though trying not to give him any clues. Which meant that she didn't feel that this was a crisis, or likely to become one. Alex only "played" like that when everything was under control. Derek felt himself relax, not even aware that he had tensed in the first place. So this stranger was a mystery, of possibly serious impact, but there was no immediate crisis.

On an otherwise quiet Friday afternoon, Derek suddenly found the idea more appealing than playing Twenty Questions with a manuscript, no matter how soothing, or allegedly dangerous. Or perhaps, he thought wryly, he was merely looking for an excuse to play hooky.

"Come on. Rachel wants you to see him before she makes any decisions about what to do with him."

Derek raised thick brown eyebrows at her words, both at the implication that the visitor needed "something done" about him, and the suggestion that the lovely, and oh-so-stubborn Doctor Rachel Corrigan would not do exactly as she deemed best, and his opinions be damned if they were not in line with her own thoughts on the matter.

Alex smiled briefly, reading the unsaid in his reaction, but she made no further comment.

"Very well." Derek heaved a sigh. "Duty calls, I suppose." With a last, involuntary look at the spread pages in front of him, Derek removed the other glove, placing them both on the table and rising from his chair.

"All right. You've managed to pique my curiosity."

Alex snorted. "Oh yeah, like that's such a difficult thing."

"Hey. Some respect, if you would."

Together, they walked down the main upstairs hallway of the Legacy House, their shoes making faint clicking noises on the wooden floor. Katherine, Rachel's twenty-year-old daughter, had been discovered sliding in her stockinged feet along the hallway last month and, rather than forbid her to do so, Derek had told the staff to stop having the floors waxed. At least until such a time as Katherine found a different amusement to occupy her time.

His mouth curled upwards slightly in secret amusement at the memory. It was good to see her acting like a normal child. The gift of Sight, that odd flicker of psychic ability she often showed, was a heavy burden to place on anyone. He and Alex, both similarly gifted, struggled with it—how much worse must it be for such a young girl facing the uncertainties of adolesence still ahead? He worried about Katherine, as he worried about all those under his care, the burden of being the head of the San Francisco Legacy house. Devoted to standing between the forces of darkness and an unsuspecting human population, the Legacy was a noble, if dangerous, calling, but the emotional and physical wear and tear it

11

left on its members could often be nothing short of crippling.

But Kat was not an official member of the team. More than that, she was at school, safely away from the House, and was not the current problem. And so he shut that concern away and focused on what was to come, channeling his energies toward what was at hand.

They descended the stairs down to the main entry foyer. Derek stopped, hesitated.

"Here. Rachel didn't want to move him too far until she had had a chance to check him out." And she indicated the heavy double wooden doors off to the left of the elegant foyer.

They slid open the doors to be greeted by the sight of a young man lying on the sofa by the dormant fireplace. He was covered with a heavy blanket, and Rachel Corrigan sat on the edge of the sofa by his side.

The blond woman looked up when they entered, and the expression on her fine-boned face was enough to put Derek on alert, his half-composed commentary about her habit of taking in strays forgotten.

"Who is this?" he asked, moving to her side and looking down at the young man—a boy, really; although he might have been in his early twenties, the impression he gave off was one of youth. He was sleeping, his face shiny as though from a fever, his forehead and jaw tight with tension as though an ugly dream pursued him.

"We don't know." Her voice was tinged with a hint of exasperation. "Jonathan found him on the doorstep just now. The mess he left behind suggests that he must have literally crawled from the beach, all the way up the steps at the front of the house"—no mean feat, considering the distance, and how many stairs there were to get from the main walkway—"and collapsed when he reached the front door. We haven't been able to wake him."

12

Derek nodded, looking down at the stranger. Dark hair, wet and slicked back against his scalp, fell to his shoulders. One ear was pierced with a strange white loop that looked like ivory instead of the typical silver or gold wire. Pale skin, a blue-white undertone that looked both genetic and enhanced, as though he had not seen the sun in some time. The cheekbones and jawline made for a well-defined face; a little on the fleshy side perhaps, but healthy-looking. But the tension of skin and muscle augured for an inner pain.

"He must have swum over, somehow," Rachel continued, drawing the blanket up around his bare shoulders. "He was soaking wet, all the way down to his bones. And besides, that's the only way he could have gotten here without being seen, or setting off any alarms."

Derek looked back at Alex, who was still standing in the doorway, talking with someone on the intercom. She nodded. "The video cameras don't show a thing, so he definitely didn't use any of the normal access routes. And nobody reported seeing a boat of any size coming near us, not even a rowboat. So I'd say swimming is a good guess."

Rachel looked down at her sleeping patient, as though imagining him making that journey, then back up at Derek. "Because of his rather . . . unorthodox manner of showing up, I wanted to get your input before I settled him in." She smiled, the expression lighting her face with mischief not unlike her daughter's, and letting him know that she knew exactly what he had been thinking about her usual decision-making mode. "Besides, we need your help lifting him. It's almost in a coma, he's sleeping so heavy, and that makes for a dead weight. And I didn't want to risk dropping him."

"Considerate of you. But you could find nothing wrong with him? Should we take him to a hospital?"

Rachel shook her head. "Physically, at least on a cursory examination, he's fine. Nothing broken, no indication of internal injuries, no contusions on the scalp. I suspect that he's just very, very tired."

"And that's not a surprise, "Alex said, coming forward now, a piece of pale green cloth in her hands. "He wasn't out for a pleasure jaunt. Look at this."

Derek took the wet fabric from her and held it out, ignoring the water which still dripped from it to fall on the expensive carpeting. "There are rips here. Tears. On the sleeve, and some on the body of the shirt. They look jagged, not like knife cuts."

"As though he was running through the brambles, maybe falling on rocks. Probably before that little swim of his, based on how both the clothing and his scrapes have been washed clean." Alex agreed.

"Running from something?"

"That's what we figured," Rachel said. "And, maybe, *to* us."

Derek nodded, thinking, his mouth pursed slightly. The Legacy House had given sanctuary to others in need before. It would not be impossible for someone in dire need of aid to hear of them through one source or another. But usually, the House would have some sort of advance warning. And generally visitors arrived in a somewhat more conventional manner. Angel Island was not easy to get to, the house even less so. The Legacy's public cover, the Luna Foundation, might be a charitable organization, but the number of well-publicized and irreplaceable works of art they were known to accumulate, house, and donate more than justified the electrified fences and electronic alarm system to anyone who might inquire.

"Fine. Then we will work with your instinct and not send him to the mainland just yet. Let's get him moved to one of the guest bedrooms. Call me if he wakes up or his condition changes. Other than that, if you think he is all right, there is nothing more we can do at the moment."

Rachel nodded in agreement. Derek motioned to Alex, ushering her out of the room and closing the door behind them.

"I don't like the fact that nobody saw him until he was literally on our front doorstep," he said. "He may be harmless. But I've gotten a little paranoid over the years. Why don't you round up Nick, see what the two of you can find out."

Alex nodded, her dark eyes serious, even when she smiled at his paranoia comment. When you dealt with the things they dealt with on a 24/7 basis, Nick was constantly reminding them paranoia was a good investment that paid healthy bonuses. Or, as he said, the question isn't 'are you paranoid?' but 'are you paranoid enough?' "

"Where is Nick, anyway? He hasn't left for the evening yet, has he?"

"Last I saw him, he was in the library. I think he was planning on spending the night."

"Catching up on his reading?" Derek asked, with a sardonic expression.

"Catching up on his snoozing, more likely," Alex retorted. "Putting that chair in the library was not one of your better ideas."

"It's a very comfortable reading chair," he said, defending himself and his favorite new addition to the House's decor.

"Too comfortable. Everyone who sits down in it loses the entire afternoon."

Derek smiled at the truth of that. "Maybe we should buy more and replace the beds in the guest rooms? Anything that lets us sleep more soundly can't be such a bad thing."

"And then have Rachel after us all about the damage we're doing to our backs? Thanks, but no thanks. I'll take my chances with insomnia."

With Derek's low chuckle from her parting shot filling the hallway behind her, Alex went in search of the fourth member of their team, Nick Boyle. She found him, as expected, asleep in the oversized brown leather chair; a newspaper open in his lap and his jaw hanging open and emitting an odd, rumbling snort that seemed perfectly in tune with the soothing atmosphere of the airy, light-filled library.

It was a nice change, she thought. Too often this room was the scene of hurried research or late-into-the-night conversations of dire import. It was nice to see someone enjoying it for more civilized, more decadent reasons.

Too bad she was going to have to put an end to it, for the moment.

"Up and at 'em, Nap Boy," she said, shaking his shoulder gently.

"What? I'm up. I'm ready. I wasn't sleeping." The ex-SEAL started, then relaxed, seeing that Alex didn't appear to be in danger, or otherwise agitated.

"What?" he asked, a little more calmly, sitting upright in the chair and rubbing his chin, where a dark shadow of five o'clock stubble had set up shop a few hours early.

"We've got company, the unexpected, unexplained kind." She shook her head at his inquiring look. "Human. Perfectly normal, no crisis. Or at least, he looks human. And out cold from exhaustion, so probably not much of a threat at the moment. But Derek wants us to find out how he got onto the island."

Yawning, Nick stood up and stretched, arms reaching for the ceiling, back arched, head tilting back slightly. Then he ran a hand through dark, rumpled hair, trying to comb it back into place. "Right," he said, looking a little more alert. "So, where do you want to start?"

16

"I want to check out the computer systems and the security cameras. He managed to get here without anyone noticing him, and somehow I don't think he just beamed down, or phased in, or whatever. Like I said, perfectly normal."

"Well, there's a change," Nick said, folding the newspaper neatly and placing it on the table. "Not that humans haven't caused us plenty of trouble before. More, sometimes, if you ask me."

Alex laughed. "That's what I love about you, Nick. Your unending and unshakeable sense of optimism."

"Hey, I happen to believe that the glass is half full. I just also strongly suspect it's leaking all over my pants." He thought about what she had told him, proccessing the information.

"Do we have anything to go on?" he asked.

"Nothing yet. I was going to correlate all the footage from the cameras, make sure that we don't have any interruptions in the coverage, and that we're not missing any time somewhere."

"Remember to take the asprin before you start, not after the headache kicks in," he reminded her. "Where was he first spotted? I'll try to backtrack from there, see if I can't find something useful."

"It shouldn't bc too hard. Just follow the puddles."

"The what?" Nick shook his head and followed her out of the library, tucking his shirt back into the waistband of his jeans. "Maybe you should start at the beginning. What do you mean by 'looks human?' "

Elsewhere in the House, Derek had returned to his office, carefully placing the manuscript in the padded wooden box it had arrived in that morning as he castigated himself for leaving it in the open like that. Even if he didn't think the book was a threat, there was no excuse for being careless.

Dismissing that lapse as nothing he could take back, he closed and locked the box, placing it on a side table. It would have to wait until this current situation was cleared up. If the boy was indeed in danger, they would need to know what kind, and from whom. The only thing worse than walking into danger was walking in without any idea what the danger was.

Or what direction it would be coming from.

With that thought in mind, he sat down at his desk, picked up the phone, and dialed a number he had long-ago memorized.

"Hello. Yes, Detective Carmack, please. Yes, I'll hold."

He waited a moment, then, "Frank? It's Derek Rayne. Yes, I know." Pause. "No, I do not only call you when I need a favor."

He smiled a little at what the man on the opposite side of the line was saying. "That's not true at all. You asked us for the favor last time."

More noise from the other side, sounding irritated.

"All right, all right, we will call it a truce, then. And yes, I'm calling to ask a favor." He paused. "Stop laughing. We had a young man appear on our front step this morning. No i.d., and I'm afraid he's out cold, so we can't ask him his name. No, Rachel seems quite sure that all he needs to do is sleep. But if I gave you his description, could you see what you could find out?"

A pause, then, "No, I think he's in need of our aid, rather than a threat. But I would feel better—yes. Thank you. White male. Looks to be in his early 20s. About 5'11", long dark brown hair, down to about his shoulders. Straight, rather untrimmed. Face is oval, a little puffy, although I suspect that we're not seeing him at his best. Nose on the largish side. Compared to whom? Give me a break, Frank."

He waited for the apology for the nose comment, then continued. "Heavy eyebrows. Dark, like his hair. I'd suspect his eyes are brown as well. Build—if he swam to the island, as we suspect, he's got to be in good shape. Not bulky, though. Built like a swimmer, or a runner. And that's about all I can give you at the moment. Once we locate the digital camera, we will e-mail you pictures, naturally. Yes, I would appreciate that. Thank you."

Derek replaced the phone carefully and sat back in his chair, staring thoughtfully at the air in front of him. He might be overreacting by bringing the police into this so quickly. The young man might be completely harmless. An innocent victim of the tides and misfortune. But he could trust Frank to keep things quiet, and it might be that the police would have useful information.

And if not, well, it wouldn't have done anyone any harm. Derek had always hated those mystery programs where the hero failed to call the police merely because to do so would have cleared up a mystery too swiftly. Real life did not require fitting twenty minutes of commercials into every hour, and he saw no reason to run his life as though it did.

He shuffled through the papers on his desk, lined up the blotter and the phone, and generally wasted time, not wanting to pick up something that would distract his subconscious from the path it was wearing on the question of their new guest. But with so little to work on, he couldn't form even the most basic of conclusions.

Fifteen minutes later, the phone rang again.

"Hello? That was quick." A pause. "Nothing? Not even a missing person's report? And the hospitals . . . No, I'm not trying to tell you how to do your job—all right. Yes, thank you. We will." A pause. "I said we would, and we will. If we discover anything about this young man that I feel you need to know, we will inform you."

Derek hung up on the detective's protests, smiling. He always kept his promises, which was why he was so careful about their wording.

But for now, it looked as though they were on their own.

Sitting back in his chair, Derek steepled his fingers and contemplated the events of the morning. It was entirely probable that this was merely a false alarm. That the young man was indeed lost, that his boat had capsized while sailing in the bay and he had found his way here, undetected, by sheer chance.

But Derek Rayne did not believe in chance. Sheer, or otherwise. Not when it came to the Legacy.

Reaching for a piece of paper stuck under the glass of his blotter, Derek picked up the phone again and dialed up the first of the Houses on his list.

"Zdravstvuyte, eto Derek Rayne iz Legacy San Francisco. U nas yest problema o kotoroy vam nuzhno znat . . ."

T W O

The guest room they had put their unexpected visitor in caught the last of the afternoon light, and the cool autumn rays came through the window, laying patterns of light and shadow on the coverlet. He had slept like the dead while Derek and Alex carried him upstairs, and barely twitched while Rachel had given him a more thorough examination, including drawing several cc's of blood to test for any abnormalities or drugs. The blood would go out with the next ferry to a lab Rachel had used in the past and knew to be both quick and discrete, while she ran her own tests on-site.

Having done everything she could for the moment, Rachel now sat in a straight-backed chair in one corner of the guest room, a hardcover book open on her lap, a steaming mug of tea cooling on the table by her side. But the book couldn't hold her attention, and she felt her eyelids sliding closed despite her best efforts.

It had been a long day, finishing the endless paperwork the Luna Foundation seemed to generate despite itself, and she had been looking forward to spending a nice quiet evening at home with her daughter. But after a hurried consultation with Derek, she had decided to stay on the island overnight to make sure that the young man didn't take a sudden turn for the worse.

Fortunately, her regular sitter was accustomed to Doctor Corrigan's "emergency" calls and was able to go over to watch Kat on such short notice, rather than Rachel having to send someone to bring her daughter back to Angel Island. Not that Kat didn't already think of the ivy-covered mansion as her second home.

The stranger stirred just then, the sheet pulled over his abused body making a rasping noise that woke Rachel from her light doze. She closed the book and placed it on the table, then rose to stand by the bedside. He was frowning in his sleep, his sweetly handsome face flexing in a rictus of pain.

Rachel checked his pulse, then felt his skin for any changes in temperature or fluid retention. Her specialization might be with the workings of the mind, but his physical state had her worried. Even allowing for the swim they were assuming he took, his exhaustion seemed somehow unnatural. It was almost as though he had been drugged, although he hadn't shown any external signs of that and the basic bloodwork she had run in the lab downstairs had come back clean.

If he didn't show more improvement soon, she'd run a second battery of tests. But if it was just exhaustion, as she suspected, then there was no need to stress his system any more. No need to invent problems before they arrived.

Although it was much easier to use the lab here than trust the results to a lab on the mainland. No matter how well-run, there was always a risk in using an outside facility. The sheer volume of tests they ran made even a simple pregnancy test a gamble in terms of accuracy.

She smiled at herself. "And you just like having a lab worth bragging about, all to yourself. Even if you can't brag to anyone about it."

The young man frowned again, whimpered once, and then his eyes opened, suddenly, with no pause from sleep to waking, and intense brown eyes focused on her face.

"Hello," she said, rearranging her face into a reassuring smile. "My name's Rachel. What's yours?"

He blinked, and his body tensed as though for flight. A sheen of perspiration broke out along the curve of his hairline.

"It's okay. You're safe. Do you know where you are?"

"Safe," he repeated, but it wasn't a question. More as though he were naming a place, a destination. His body relaxed somewhat, settling back into the mattress.

"Yes. You're safe here." She paused, studying him, then continued in a quiet voice. "Do you remember how you got here?"

"Swam." His voice was husky, thick, as though he had not spoken in a very long time and had forgotten the mechanics of pronunciation.

"That's a very long swim you took, then. Unless you fell off a boat?"

He shook his head, turning his face wearily into the pillow and fading back off to sleep. Rachel couldn't tell if he was really that exhausted or merely didn't want to answer any more questions. Probably a little of both. Or a lot of both, if he really had swum here from the coast.

She stepped back, staring at the body in the bed. Perhaps she should have taken him to a hospital on the mainland. But things which occurred here, in her mind, tended to fall under the heading of "Legacy business," not to be opened up to anyone outside that select group. And Derek had agreed, which sealed the matter.

Before joining the Legacy, Rachel Corrigan had been a level-headed practicalist. She had believed that the best way to deal with things was to bring them out in the open, where they could be examined and healed. It was why she went into psychiatry in the first place. Everything, even the terrible accidental death of her husband and son, was to be dealt with in as straightforward and open a manner as possible. That way you gave the demons no place to hide.

But that was before she discovered that some demons were more of the flesh than the mind. And that the damage they could do, if let loose among innocents, was terrible.

No, best to keep him here. At least until they determined what had driven him to such a headlong flight. Better to be overcautious than sorry.

And Kat would understand. At ten, she wasn't quite old enough yet to understand all of what the Legacy was and why it demanded so much of her mother's time, but she did know that what was done here was important, and that sometimes emergencies happened.

"Are you an emergency?" she asked him softly. "Or are we getting all nervous over a wayward tourist?"

But the young man, sound asleep again, gave no answer.

A few minutes before the small alarm clock ticked over to five P.M., the door creaked open a handspan, and Alex stuck her head in. She saw Rachel staring thoughtfully into the empty air of the room.

"Hey."

"Oh. Hi. Security detail done?"

The younger woman grinned. "I finished off my side of it, anyway. Nick's still out there doing the grunt work. He was supposed to just do a quick once-over, then come back and help me with the security scan, but you know Nick. He's happier when he's doing something more active than poking at a terminal screen. Makes him feel like a real man, not a desk jockey."

The two women shared a smile at the expense of their co-worker, then Alex came all the way inside the room and indicated their visitor with a jerk of her pointed chin. "Sleeping Beauty wake up yet?"

"For about thirty seconds, and then was back out. He speaks English, at least. And we were right, he did swim here. God alone knows how, that's an awfully long swim. And he's not exactly in marathon shape. Not that he's unhealthy—his vitals are sound as a horse's, except for his extreme exhaustion."

"What about the bruising on his skin? That looked pretty bad."

Rachel nodded. "They look to be of recent origin, as though he was in a terrible fight no more than three or four days ago. I'd guess he won, from the lack of more serious injuries. But it must have been one heck of a fight. Just the way he reacted when I told him that he was safe . . ." Rachel's voice trailed off. His skittishness was that of an abused animal, which corroborated with the marks she had found on his skin. But his hands showed damage that could only come from landing blows, as well. So whatever had been done to him, he hadn't been a helpless victim.

"I wonder if I made the right decision in keeping him here. Maybe he would be better off under a specialist's care."

Alex looked at him, a long, judging gaze, then shook her head. "No, I don't think so. You're just getting into a jag of second-guessing yourself."

Rachel made a "who me?" gesture.

"Yes, you. I think that you were right with your first instinct. In any other case I would say yes, maybe we should have brought him to the emergency room, just to be on the safe side, but I don't think we should take him off the island."

Hearing her own vague thoughts echoed in the other woman's words made Rachel sit up straight and forget to speak softly. "What? Was there something on the tapes, or—Alex, do you See something?"

Derek, as Precept, made his decisions based on Legacy guidelines, what was best for the good of all, not necessarily the one. But Alex's reactions were closer to the individual—closer to Rachel's own, both as physician and as person.

The younger woman put a finger to her lips, glancing at the body motionless in the bed, then made a gesture of uncertainty and dropped her hand back to her side. "I don't know. There's just something in the air . . ."

The two women looked at each other, both aware that hunches and "weird feelings" which might be discounted by others were as valid here as spreadsheets and market reports were to other professions.

Alex's expression was concerned. "I don't know anything for certain, Rachel. But whatever made him come here, whatever chased him so badly that he was willing to risk drowning . . . I think it's still out there. Waiting for him."

Nick was singing. He wasn't more than an enthusiastic singer at the best of times, and the cool night air wasn't doing much for his vocal cords. But he kept at it, more out of determination to finish than enjoyment. One more verse, and then he could give up without shame.

Tilting his head back, he scanned the horizon. It was promising to be one of those early autumn nights that are usually reserved for New England: crisp, clear, and dry. To the west, the last streaks of red and blues were fading, and a full heaven of stars was beginning to glimmer in the eastern sky. They would have to battle the light pollution from the city and the softer lights already coming from the house behind him to shine, but somehow they always managed to. A miracle of nature, and worth the hassle of the Legacy being situated out here, instead of at a more central location.

Jumping a low fence, Nick walked down a gentle slope, his eyes scanning for anything unusual. Yeah, definitely a pretty night. It could have been a little warmer, but overall, he had no complaints. Except, of course, that he thought he was wasting his time.

The water lapped up against the shoreline, cut by the cough-and-mutter of a powerboat in the distance and an occasional low-pitched bark of a sea lion carrying across the water. He had found the promised puddle of water on the stairs and managed to track the kid's trail back to the waterline, where he'd obviously pulled himself out, based on the drag-marks still visible in the sand. Maybe a blind man couldn't have found the trail, but it was definitely basic cub scout material.

Okay, so it was odd that the kid didn't trip any of their cameras and that he got all the way to the house without anyone seeing him. But things like that happened. No spookiness or supernatural causes required. And while the system here was good—he knew, he helped design it   there's no way it was military class. Not even close.

In Nick's opinion, they should have used the 'copter to airlift the kid to the hospital on the mainland, asked to be posted on updates, and gone home. There wasn't any reason to keep him here, and a lot of reasons— namely his condition—to get him checked out by a full facility.

"But hey, I'm just go-for-coffee-boy tonight," he muttered, giving up on the last chorus as he completed his circuit of the beachfront. "Nobody asks my opinion for anything."

That wasn't quite fair, actually. Derek's decision wasn't anything so unusual, just being his typical ultra-cautious self when it came to the Legacy's well-being.

Deciding that poking around any more in the growing dusk wouldn't be worth the effort, he shoved his hands into his jacket pocket to warm them up and cut back over the bluff to return to the house. The only thing on his mind was getting a cup of coffee and some dinner inside him. After all, what did it matter if the kid spent the night with them? At least they weren't going to hassle him for insurance cards and next-of-kin information. One night they'd make sure nothing's up and then he could fly the 'copter over in the morning and drop him off on the mainland. No biggie.

The closer he got to the house, the more reasonable that logic seemed. And by the time he reached the edge of the lawn, he had forgotten his initial reluctance in the overwhelming desire to get inside and get warm.

When enumerating my many faults, Sloan has always claimed that I should never be left alone with my thoughts, that they will merely lead me into trouble. Though I would never admit it to him, it may be that he is correct. These past few weeks have been quiet, quieter than it has been in months and I had been, perhaps subconsciously, looking for something to come along and break the routine.

I should have learned by now that wishes are often answered, not as we might desire, but as we might fear.

Derek placed his pen down and raised his head to stare out the window, not seeing anything other than his interior landscape of thoughts and misgivings. If nothing else, he had learned over the years to listen to his instincts, to his gut feelings. And right now, his gut was unsettled.

There was nothing that he could pinpoint, nothing to

pin down and say "this is what is wrong." But somehow a sense of foreboding had come into the house with their young visitor. Not so much a shadow as a feather-light touch sweeping across his awareness and gone again the moment you became conscious of it.

"Sloan *was* right. You are looking for trouble," he chided himself. "As though it doesn't show up often enough on its own." And yet . . .

With a shake of his head, Derek picked up his pen again and finished his journal entry.

I can feel something, a pricking in my thumbs. Whether paranoia or common sense or a foresight, I cannot tell. For the moment, the future is blind. But whatever has chased this young man to us, we can do no less than follow it through to the end. That is our charge, to aid those in need. And whatever else may come, I suspect he will need all the help we can muster.

He capped the pen and closed the journal. His stomach rumbled, and only then did he realize how late it had gotten. Night had fallen, and his eyes were strained from trying to read without a light. Standing, he stretched, wincing as he heard bones crack, and then his stomach followed up with an unhappy rumble. He had missed lunch, working on the manuscript, and now this business had caused him to forgo dinner.

"Food, first. Then trouble."

Across the water, the lights of San Francisco began to turn on, glittering their defiance to the deepening dusk. The mist which never seemed far from the city's shores crept inward with the tide, lying low and inoffensive. A normal evening in the City by the Bay.

But a little farther out, off a sharp cliff overlooking the blue-gray Pacific waters, a heavier patch of fog had formed. Ten-feet high, and almost half-a-mile wide, it was flat on the bottom and jagged at the top. In the half-light it seemed almost as though tiny lights flickered within it, a silent counterclockwise maelstrom in an otherwise stable formation. Any meteorologist worth his or her salt would have been thumbing through their books, trying to identify the weather conditions which would cause a stand-alone condition like that to rise up so suddenly.

But while such a theoretical forecaster was researching, the formation moved out to sea, surging forward like a ship under sail. Or, if one's imagination were allowed an opinion, like a pack of riders on unruly steeds made of some substance not quite solid, not quite real.

And only a particularly careful observer—of which there were none on that empty bluff—would have noted that the fog was moving directly against the wind. Directly across the water toward a small island marked on the county maps as ANGEL ISLAND—PRIVATE PROPERTY.

THREE

Even with this new puzzle to chew at, the business of the Legacy still went on. The lines carrying information hummed back and forth, from island to mainland and back again. Paperwork was filed, supply lists made, and bills were paid. Ordinary work that was the lifeblood of even the most supernatural of organizations.

With the Legacy occupied in that manner, the rest of the evening passed. Night fell completely, and the windows of the great stone mansion glimmered with lights against the darkness as the inhabitants went on with their work undeterred. Alex was sitting in the chair by one such light, working on her laptop computer, when their mysterious stranger finally woke up again. He stirred, pushing the sheet away restlessly, then turned his head to meet her inquisitive gaze. Two pairs of brown eyes met, and held.

"Hello." Her hair was loose now, and it fell to her shoulders in a tangle of black corkscrew curls that she despaired of ever taming. Tucking a particularly annoying lock behind one ear, she studied the young man for a moment, then stood up slowly, putting the laptop down on the seat she had vacated.

Rachel had given her a full briefing on the results of her examination when she took over the night watch, and Alex's own observations now were written to the mental file she was forming labeled "Doe, John." But nothing added up, not yet.

Moving the way one would to keep from frightening a cornered animal, she walked closer to the side of the bed.

"You're . . . not who was here before." He winced at the croaking noise that emerged. She took a glass of water from the table beside the bed and lifted it to his mouth, supporting his head with her other hand, until a slow trickle of the clear liquid had moistened his mouth and tongue. "Better?"

He nodded, watching her cautiously, as though he expected to be kicked for expressing an opinion.

"No, that was Rachel," she answered his earlier question. "I'm Alex. And you are . . . ?" She waited, and a puzzled look crossed his face, as though he was uncertain of the answer.

Amnesia? she wondered. Rachel had said that might be a possibility. But he didn't have the panicked look amnesia victims often had when they realized they couldn't remember anything. Their mystery guest looked more . . . comforted. As though he had forgotten a terrible dream, rather than his own name. *Interesting*, as Derek would say.

"I . . . David." His voice gathered strength as he settled on the name like a talisman. "My name is David."

Well, that was a start. "David what?"

His newfound confidence deflated slowly, and the abused-puppy look returned, making Alex sorry that she had pushed the question. "I . . . don't know. I . . ."

Amnesia of some sort, then. With luck it would just be temporary, from the strain he had put on his body in getting here. Rachel would be able to better judge. Tomorrow. There was no need to call the other woman in now, no reason to put him through the rigors of another examination. He was probably still in shock, that's why he was reacting so oddly. The poor kid. The psychic felt a wave of compassion overriding her natural curiosity and the hesitation of earlier.

"Shhh. It's okay. It will come back to you." Alex smiled sympathetically. "You've had a tough time of it, haven't you?"

He nodded, then shrugged, vacillating helplessly between reactions and emotions before shutting everything behind a bland facade.

"You took quite a knock on the head, I'd guess." She reached forward to touch his forehead where a new purple-green bruise had formed, but stopped when she noticed that his body had tensed at her approach. So, he didn't like to be touched. More information to be filed away in the hope that it would be useful. If nothing else, it indicated the kind of treatment he had been subjected to.

Poor kid, she thought again. Maybe that was what she was picking up, the ugliness he had run from. That kind of scarring left tracks a mile wide, once you knew what to look for.

Letting her hand slowly down to rest at her side, she tilted her head and smiled again in what she hoped was a non-threatening fashion. "Do you know where you are?"

David shook his head no, now-dry hair falling forward into his face. He needed a haircut: from the uneven lengths and ragged edges, he had been hacking it off with a penknife. Had he been living on the streets, perhaps? That would explain some of it, if not why he was still so afraid. And not why he had come to the Legacy, specifically.

"You're safe here," she reassured him. "We just want to help you. And no," she added, "we're not the government. So no fear of any annoying paperwork to be filled out in triplicate." She made a self-deprecating gesture with her hands, to indicate that she was joking. His face remained impassive, but she thought that she saw a crinkling around his tired brown eyes that indicated recognition, at least, of the humor.

He shoved his hair back absently with one hand, pulling the heavy length behind his head into an untied ponytail with what was obviously a habitual motion, and tried to sit up. But it was too soon, and he collapsed back onto the pillows with a muscle-weary groan.

"Hey, hang on, okay?" She reached behind him, adjusting the pillows so that they supported him. "Better?"

He nodded, looking up at her with an unexpectedly shy smile that completely transformed his face from ordinary to heart-stopping. *So he does have more than one expression*, she thought, responding almost against her will to his charm with an unforced smile of her own.

"Thank you. Truth, I'm feeling about as strong as a string bean." His voice firmed as he used it, and Alex noted the characteristic vowel sounds of Eastern New England. Something to use in finding out who he was. Or should they let him try to remember for himself? She would have to ask Rachel what she thought best. Although Derek, of course, would be for finding out everything they could, as fast as they could. Rachel had often said that when he was focused on something, his bedside manner was enough to make autopsy victims try to get out of bed.

"Okay. You hang right there, and I'll get you something to eat, to build that strength back up. Some soup,

I think. Your stomach won't take much more than that. Don't go anywhere, now."

"I won't. Promise."

The woman with coffee-colored skin and the gentle voice left the room, and David relaxed back into the pillows supporting his upper body, his smile fading. His eyes were shadowed with pain, and an intense, exhausted worry that had little to do with his physical condition.

Something was wrong in his head. Things were ... missing. Things he should have known if not on waking, then soon after. Where was he? Who were they, these women? And how had he gotten here?

He closed his eyes, scrunching his face in concentration as he tried to recall anything, anything at all. But his memory seemed to be filled with a dark haze, swirling and shifting and threatening. Blinding light into grunge gray; a delicate smile; laughter and music that turned cold and tinny; the sugar rush of panic; the pain of desire ...

No!

Then the shadows parted, just a sliver, and a cattle prod of memory came back to him. Opening his eyes, David stared at the wall in front of him. His skin was hot, flushed, and his pulse raced from just that effort. And the reward had been a memory so horrible that he wasn't sure if he wanted to dredge the fog for more or burrow back into his amnesia and forget what little he did recall.

But somehow, he knew that it wasn't going to be that easy. He wouldn't be allowed to escape from what he had seen. From what he knew. From what had been.

"Ashanon," he whispered, regret and disgust balanced in his voice, as though biting into a peach filled with wormwood.

Ashanon. His voice felt fuzzy, heavy, echoing with too many layers. Like a synesthesiacs' fever dream, the word brought a wave of colors and scents, textures and sounds twined together in deliberate chaos. It made his head swell, his sinuses freeze, his eyes implode from the pressure. And he knew that if he could just swim to the middle, allow it to sink into him and become a part of him again, the pattern would separate out, and all the pieces would fall into place.

The thought was terrifying. Impossible. Better to remain blind forever than to see clearly what waited for him.

David shook off those thoughts. *Deal with what's now, you idiot. Deal with what you can handle.* If he craned his neck just so, he could see through the room's one window, its three-paned glass unobstructed now by screen or shade. The sky outside the window was dark, and he could see the branches of evergreen trees dip and sway in a faint breeze. And again he wondered: how long had he been here? How long had he been asleep, unguarded?

And who were these people who had taken him in? Could they be trusted?

Would they protect him?

Could they protect him?

He shuddered like a horse shaking off flies and forced himself to close his eyes and relax. They had to. He had come here, been led here, for a reason.

They had to protect him. Because he couldn't go back. Not ever. Not while there was still breath in him to resist.

"He's awake."

Alex's announcement caught Derek sitting at the kitchen table with a coffee mug halfway to his mouth. He arrested the movement, looking up to meet her gaze, his own expression questioning. Despite the lateness of the hour, he was still wide awake, if somewhat rumpled looking. Alex snorted at her internal criticisms, knowing that she looked not much better. Joining the Legacy meant that you pretty much gave up all hope of something resembling normal working hours. Most days she preferred that. Years of school had honed night owl tendencies, until now she generally came into her best working hours after ten at night.

As for Derek, well, back in the days she had known him only as Professor Rayne, she had seen him work around the clock for days at a time, relentlessly pursuing some fact, some final conclusion. It was almost as though he forgot that his body was flesh and didn't feel the need for sleep.

After joining the Legacy to work by his side, it had been a tremendous relief to discover that he maintained a continuous consumption of caffeine to present that impression. It was nice, after a really tough investigation, to see the line of coffee mugs he left in his wake, a reminder that he was only mortal like the rest of them.

But still, some awe remained. To the casual observer, Derek Rayne might be the ordinary man on the street. Tall, he was good-looking without being handsome, noticeable without being memorable. His graying brown hair was shaggy in a way that suggested that he had forgotten to get it cut, and his face in repose reminded her of nothing so much as drawings she had seen of the lion Aslan, from C.S. Lewis's Narnia books: noble, but worn down.

But his eyes . . . Like Aslan, when you looked into his eyes, the awe came rushing back. Intellect, yes, undoubtedly. Charisma as well. But even more, there was wisdom in those heavy-set eyes. A wisdom they all relied upon, every day, and in every crisis.

And now, unsure, she turned to that source again.

"I think you should talk to him. I know that Rachel said he was fine, except for some knocks and scrapes and exhaustion, only . . . He had trouble remembering his name, couldn't recall his last name at all. But there's more than amnesia working here, Derek. There's something bothering him. Something he's afraid of, so that a loss of memory is almost a relief."

"Is that a reasoned judgment, or . . ."

Alex shook her head, shoving her hands into the back pockets of her jeans. "I don't think so. No. It's just . . . a feeling. Rachel may be right, there's something not kosher here. He's got some weird vibes going on."

A new voice broke in before Derek could respond. "Great. Just what we need around here, more weird vibes."

The two turned to look as Nick came into the kitchen, rubbing his hands together briskly. He was wearing thick grey sweatpants and a leather jacket over a sweatshirt, with knit gloves sticking out of one pocket. The tips of his ears and nose were pink from the wind, and his short dark hair was disheveled.

"Cold out?" Alex asked.

"Funny." He ha-ha'd in her direction.

"I thought you were going to the mainland for the night," Derek said, surprised.

"I was. I was just giving the immediate perimeter another go-round before I called it a night." He shrugged. "And then I realized it was too late to head back anyway, and . . ."

"And you'd forgotten to call your date and tell her you'd be late?"

"I left her a message," Nick defended himself. "Anyway, it looks clear. Nothing on the sensors, and I didn't feel so much as a rise in my hackles, except from the fact that it's getting cold there. So, what's this about vibes, weird or otherwise?"

38

"Our guest has awoken, according to Alex. I was just about to go upstairs and introduce myself."

"You want some company?" he offered, taking off his jacket and draping it over the back of a chair.

"No, I think it would be best if we did not overwhelm him just now. Alex and I will see what he can tell us about his unexpected arrival."

"Right." Nick turned the chair around and sat down in it, leaning his arms on the ladder back and propping his chin on his arms. "I'll just stay down here and guard the coffee, then."

Derek smiled briefly, holding his mug away from Nick as he got up from the table. "You do that. With your own mug."

"And heat up some soup for David while you're down here, okay?" Alex requested. "There should be some soup in the freezer you can defrost in the microwave. Rachel said we should get some liquids into him as soon as he woke up."

"David, huh? Liquids. Right. I can handle nuking something. Probably." He made a pitiful face, ignoring the fact that they both knew that he was more than bachelor-capable in the kitchen.

"We have faith in you," she said, patting him on the shoulder as she left the room on Derek's heels.

David had managed to wrest himself to an upright sitting position by the time they returned and was looking around the room with undisguised curiosity. The sheet had slipped further down his body, revealing a bare, hairless chest covered with the faint white cris-crossing of long-healed scars. Alex, stepping inside the room and taking up position by the door, had the glazed-eye look that meant she was carefully avoiding any reaction to the sight, but her jaw tightened.

Derek also noted the scars, as well as Alex's reaction

to them, but was more interested in the way the young man's eyes flicked over certain objects, and rested almost reverently on others. Pictures, objects d'art, furniture, all dismissed. Electronics as simple as the alarm clock on the table by the side of the bed, or the laptop Alex had left open on her chair, seemed the focus of an almost longing intensity. And the mirror hanging on the wall over the dresser—David seemed fascinated by his reflection and yet disturbed by it as well, if the way his gaze flickered to it and then away quickly was any indication. Interesting.

Even more interesting was the way he reacted to Derek's entrance: shock, followed quickly by relief. Directed toward Derek himself, obviously, but why? Because he was an authority figure? Or because he was male?

"So. Welcome to the Luna Foundation," he said. There was not a flicker of recognition on the boy's face. "My name is Derek Rayne, and you have already met Alex, yes?"

David nodded, that smile lighting his face again and making him seem even younger than Derek had first guesstimated. "And there was a woman before, a blond woman? Rachel?"

"Yes. Rachel Corrigan. She's a doctor, she examined you when you first arrived. You gave us quite a scare, I must say. And left us with some unanswered questions. Like how you managed to arrive on the island without anyone seeing you." He waited, then, when no response was forthcoming, asked directly. "Do you remember how you got here, David?"

The young man's smile fled, his face in repose taking on a slack, almost pouting quality that seemed to be his natural expression. "I . . . no. Like I told Alex, I can't remember much of anything. And I've been trying."

"What do you remember? It's all right, you can tell

me. We're not here to harm you. We want to help. But first you must tell us everything you can remember." Derek's normally seductive voice had taken an even more soothing quality, as though inviting everyone within hearing to relax into it. Bad bedside manner or not, when he wanted something from you, Derek could be as hypnotic as the swaying of a cobra. David, apparently, was not immune. He sat up, painfully, leaning almost involuntarily toward the older man.

"I . . . I was being chased. A gang . . . a lot of voices, angry voices. They had hurt me. It was a game with them, I think. To hurt me, make me do things. But I . . . escaped." There was a note of pride in his voice at that. "I got away from them. But they found me. I was running. Through the woods." He frowned, trying desperately to remember. "I was afraid. If they caught me, it would have been bad. Very bad. I fell, hurt myself." He paused. "Then there was water, and I knew that if I could get out there . . . if I could reach the light, the warm place, I would be safe . . ."

Derek turned back to Alex, who shrugged, his questions mirrored in her dark eyes. "He may have some latent psychic ability that allowed him to sense us here, if he truly was in danger," she said quietly, not moving from her location by the door.

Derek nodded, returning his attention to their guest. "And this gang, why were they chasing you?"

"I . . ." David swallowed, his face becoming even paler. "I don't know."

"You don't remember?" Derek's voice was carefully neutral, but anyone who knew him would have recognized the sudden tension in his body. For whatever reason, David's words didn't have the ring of complete truth to them. But Derek forced his shoulders to relax, willing himself not to spook the boy further. If he truly could not remember, pressing him would be counterproductive.

David sank back onto the bed, the spell of Derek's voice clearly broken. "No. I . . . I can't remember anything before . . . " He stopped, swallowed heavily. "Like I said, there are flashes, little bits of memory. They had me chained," and his hand lifted to his neck, which did indeed show faint marks of a collar of some sort, long faded. "Like a pet. A toy. But I don't know why. *I can't remember*."

"Well," Derek said, forcing a smile to his face that he didn't feel. "There's time for that. Perhaps a little more rest and something to eat will help your memory."

"I can stay here, then?" David's voice was almost too eager, and he looked down at his hands, abashed. "I . . . I can be useful. I'm a good worker. I can cook and clean. And any chores you have that need doing . . . "

Alex had started slightly as he spoke, her eyes narrowing as she looked at him. Derek gave her a sharp look but didn't comment on it.

"We can worry about all of that later, all right? For now, rest. Someone will bring soup up in just a little while, and you are to eat all of it and not worry about whatever happened. Your memory will come back sooner if you do not push at it."

"Okay," David agreed, as docile as a child. But there was something in his eyes that made Alex hesitate by the doorway before closing the door gently behind her.

"Derek?"

"Shhh." He held up a finger, then took her elbow and led her away from the room. Going down the stairs, they met Nick coming up with a bowl of steaming soup, a spoon, napkins, and a handful of crackers on a tray.

"Hey. Done already?"

"Alex was correct, he is not quite coherent yet. Leave the soup where he can reach it, and come downstairs and join us in the office, if you would, please."

"Sure."

By the time Nick came back downstairs, Derek was back on the phone with the local police department. Nick raised an eyebrow, and was waved into a chair. He sat on the edge of the desk instead, leaning over Alex's shoulder as she ran a database search.

"So, what did you think?"

"About David?" Nick thought for a minute. "Didn't really have time to make much of a judgment. Seemed like an okay kid. Not much of a talker, awake or asleep. A little jumpy, though. Somebody wailed on him, but good." The young man's voice was hard when he said that, and Alex looked up from the screen in immediate, unspoken sympathy.

"You okay?" They both knew what she was referring to. Only his closest friends knew that Nick's own father had taken out his frustrations and anger on his own family, and although the physical marks had faded long ago, Nick still bore the results within himself.

"Yeah. He just looks so . . . helpless, lying there. Those scars, they're from a whip of some kind, or maybe a switch. Not too long ago, either. Year, tops."

"That's what Rachel said, too."

"You think whoever he was running from did that?"

Alex shrugged. "I don't know. Maybe. Probably."

Nick tapped his fingers against his denim-clad thigh, a restless movement that indicated his state of mind. If someone were to come knocking, what would be their most means of attack? Maybe he should take another look at the monitors, just to make sure Alex hadn't messed up something when she pulled the files . . .

"I wish he could have told us something more about that gang that was chasing him; why he was caught up with them, how long they held him," Alex continued.

"I know that stress can damage memories, black out traumatic events, but there's something about him, Nick. Something . . . off." She paused. "Or maybe it's not about him, but *around* him. Does that make any sense whatsoever?"

"No. But we're used to that from you."

"Gee, thanks."

Derek hung up the phone and turned his chair so that he was facing them. "Well, knowing his name didn't turn up anything on the police records either. Alex? You seemed to have something to say upstairs. What is it?"

"I'm not sure. Like I was just saying to Nick, there was something, especially when he was talking about the gang . . ." She frowned, her face scrunching in concentration. "It's familiar, but I can't remember where I've encountered it before. Or how I'm even sensing it now."

"Hmm. Interesting. If you recall anything further, let me know." Then Derek seemed to shake that thought off. "Let's work with what we do have. A young man, about twenty years old, would you say?"

The two looked at each other, nodded.

"Mental state: confused, yet coherent. Possible amnesia. Alex, how did he appear to you?"

She frowned. "Like you said, a little confused. Shaky, maybe a little gun-shy. Hesitant. He didn't want to be touched. But not surprising, really. All things considered."

"Nick?"

Nick looked at Alex, then shook his head. "I didn't see anything like that. In fact, he almost—it was weird, actually. I sort of touched him on the shoulder, you know, when I left the soup with him, just because he seemed like he needed it, and he leaned into that like a horse that likes being groomed. You know what I mean?"

"Yes. I suspect that I do. Our young friend seems to have a slight hesitation around women. Interesting. Now, physically, I think things are a bit more black and white. According to Rachel, he is in rather good shape, despite a pattern of scarring on his back, chest and arms, indicating past abuse. Anything else to add?" The two shook their heads.

"Now, he claims to have been chased by a gang of some sort."

"But he doesn't remember who they were, or why they were chasing him," Nick added.

"So he says."

Nick looked at Derek, then at Alex. "You think he was lying? Why?"

"Lying is a rather strong word. Say rather, he was not in—what do you call it, Nick? Total share mode? As to why—that, I suspect, is something we will not know until we find out who our mysterious David actually is. Alex, run a search through the Legacy database; perhaps they will have better results than the local authorities."

She nodded.

"Not difficult," Nick snorted, then subsided when Derek gave him a look. "Right. And I get to . . . ?"

"Go over the security records, every tape and sensor monitor, for any aberration, any indication that they might have been tampered with. I know that you've looked at them already. Do it again." He softened his voice, aware that he was asking them to go over work they had already done, like erring schoolchildren. "Before, we were working under the assumption that he might have been washed up here by accident. But from what he has said, and taking Alex's feelings into account, I think we need to start thinking of this as official Legacy business, with the potential dangers attached. Check again with everyone who was on duty during the time period we estimate he washed up on the island. I

45

want to know how he arrived on our very doorstep without anyone being the wiser."

"Right." Nick got up, and headed out the door. But before leaving he stopped, turning around with a determined expression on his face.

"Derek. Someone beat on him pretty bad . . ."

"And if we find them," the head of the Legacy agreed, "we will take steps to prevent it from happening again."

Nick nodded once, satisfied, and left the office.

Derek stared after him for a long moment, concerned. There was still a great deal of anger in Nick from his own painful childhood, and this situation seemed to be bringing much of that to the surface. Still, it might not be such a bad thing. If their guest felt more comfortable around men, then that was the tack they would take. Perhaps Nick, with his similar background, would have better luck in getting David to remember what had happened, by getting him to talk through it.

And perhaps it would be healing for Nick as well.

In the guest room upstairs, David put aside the bowl of half-eaten soup with a grimace. If nothing else, he had remembered that he didn't like tomato soup.

Suddenly anxious, he forced himself to sit up and swing his legs over the side of the bed, wincing as his bare feet touched the floor. He picked up one foot, twisting and holding it steady so he could see the cuts and bruising on his sole. Obviously, his boots were history.

No great loss, he thought, placing both feet gently down on the floor again to test his reactions. The man, with his graying shock of hair and lined face, had told him to feel at home, to consider himself safe here. Had offered him sanctuary, with intent if not in so many words.

But without the words, without the words spoken before witnesses, to bind him to his promise . . . Somehow he knew that was important, part of the rules of the game—

No. It didn't matter. The man was mortal, almost overwhelmingly so, which meant that his word could be trusted without oaths. No cruel traps, laid with silken webs and sharp biting humor that was meant to wound.

Ashanon . . .

David stood, and winced again, this time as his muscles screamed at the activity. But he persevered, padding naked over to the window. He moved slowly and somewhat hunched over, but he could feel the blood stirring in his veins again. When he reached the glass, he leaned on the frame and looked outside. From there, he could see a wider vista than had been available from the bed. In the distance, the lights of San Francisco flickered and danced.

But closer, on the water, other lights flickered as well. Green and gold and red dancing lights, tiny flickers like fireflies or a shaking of confetti. David watched them, his jaw set.

"You can't have me," he told them as they drew closer in a circular, weaving fashion. "You can't have me any more. Do you hear me? No more! I'm protected now."

But his voice had a hopeful quality, as though he were hoping what he said was true, rather than being assured of it.

As though in response, the lights flared scarlet, the color of fresh blood, rising higher off the water before sinking low again, almost out of sight on the waterline. A challenge, as clear as if it had been spoken in words.

FOUR

Alex turned on her side, mumbling softly under her breath as some dream chased through her subconscious. A sudden jerk of her legs, tangled with the covers, and she awoke without realizing there had been a shift from dream to consciousness. One instant she had been completely asleep, the next almost hyperaware, a transition that was unusual for her. Normally, she staggered to alertness in slow steps, fighting it all the way. But it was far too early to be awake, not even dawn yet, from the shadowed light coming in through her window. She hadn't realized, when she chose this room, that it had an eastern exposure. And once settled in, she had been too lazy to move again. Besides, it was a nice room. She liked it. Except for times like now.

Nick had taken over what he flippantly dubbed "Operation David-watch" a little after midnight. After leaving the two men making cautious small talk, she had checked in with Derek, still reading in the library. With nothing new to report, the conversation had been brief. She then had staggered off to her own room, barely kicking off her shoes and shedding her jeans before crawling into bed. Now, forced awake, she felt as though she had merely closed her eyes for a second, and was possibly even more tired than she had been before.

She groaned, rolling onto her back. The ceiling stared back at her. Somehow, the white painted surface seemed aware, almost accusing.

"You're projecting, Alexandra."

She closed her eyes, rolled back onto her side, and tried to force herself back into sleep.

Not a chance. She opened her eyes and glared at the window.

A curl fell over her forehead, into her eyes, and she reached up to catch it between two fingers, twirling it absently, closing her eyes again and listening to nothing. The house was silent in the pre-dawn, no sounds of the settling or creaking endemic in old houses.

And yet . . .

Her heart thrummed unevenly against her rib bone, warning of something off-kilter. Like a deer spooked, she waited in the pre-dawn grayness, anticipating something unknown about to happen. It was too quiet. As though someone had thrown a switch and shut off all noise. Was that what had woken her? The silence? Or had there been something else? Something that had stopped when she awoke?

She reached out with her mental senses, but felt nothing. Less than nothing, as though a wet cotton pad had been placed over her, cutting everything off, but gently. It wasn't necessarily anything to worry about; a bad cold could do the same thing to her. The Gift was unpredictable, if it was anything. And yet . . .

She pursed her lips, let out a puff of air just to make

sure sound still existed, then laughed at herself, at her sudden fear.

Silly.

And yet, perhaps not so silly.

Not when you were a part of the Legacy.

"Great," she whispered. "Just great."

Sitting up slowly, she pushed her feet into slippers waiting by the side of the bed and reached for her robe, which was thrown across the back of the chair by her bed. Belting it around her securely, she walked to the door and reached for the knob, hesitating just before her fingers closed on it.

"Come on, Alex. What's gotten you so spooked?" She scolded herself but still hesitated. Did she really believe that there would be a monster out in the hallway waiting to grab her? She was a child of the 90s, alert to the realities of science and nature, aware of the twin dangers of superstition and gullibility.

But she was also a member of the Legacy, and she knew that the monsters were sometimes very real.

"Grow some spine!" she could hear Nick telling her. "Nothing out there but your own imagination."

Gathering her courage, she opened the door and walked out into the hallway. Nothing there. Her slippers made a shush-shushing noise on the wooden floor, but other than that, the house was almost unnaturally still. Even at this hour of the morning, there should have been some noises. Although the house was solidly built, the sound of water running carried throughout the building, and when Nick was in the kitchen directly below her, you could hear him clear into the next county, banging cabinet doors shut and slamming drawers.

"Hello?"

A sudden thump behind her made her jump, turning around, one hand flat against her chest.

"I'm sorry, I didn't mean to startle you."

It was Derek, fully dressed, and looking as though he hadn't slept. And probably he hadn't. His shirt was rumpled, and the dark blue cardigan he had put on had items stashed in the pockets, perhaps picked up in his absent rambles through the house as he thought. The very normality of it made her heart settle into a more relaxed pace.

"You're smiling," he noted, putting his hands in those overloaded pockets and looking steadily at her.

"Um. Nothing. I was just wondering . . ."

"If I've been to sleep yet?"

"Yes." A beat, a fond smile. "Have you?"

"Briefly." He smiled back, the faintest upward curl of full lips lighting his brown eyes with affection. "You were right, that new chair is most seductive."

"Derek . . ." *Don't be such a pain*, her tone said.

A sudden crash broke into their banter and made Alex jump once again. In her concern over the dark shadows under her mentor's eyes, she had almost forgotten the question of what had woken her in the first place.

The crash came again, and then a wailing alarm synchronized with the flash of lights hidden in the molding along the hallway ceilings at measured intervals. Heavy thumps sounded against the walls, like the tentative slapping of a cat's paw, magnified a million times.

"Damn," Derek muttered, turning and heading down the hallway at a pace that belied his evident exhaustion. Bewildered, Alex followed him, even as she heard doors slamming open throughout the house. Rachel came out of a room at the other end of the hallway, pulling a sweater over her head, reappearing with tousled hair and a worried expression. "I'm going to check on David," she shouted over the din, moving past them. Derek nodded and continued down the stairs

"What's going on?" Alex demanded, catching up with him again. She had heard that alarm only once before, when Nick had installed it after that little incident with the spirits of a Scottish clan who had come back as tools of the Darkside. Alex still had nightmares about being trapped in the basement, watching the lights go out one by one. . . .

"We're under attack," Derek informed her tersely, reaching the bottom of the stair and heading for the library and the room that housed the heart of the Legacy.

"I kind of figured that," she said with exasperation. "But by whom?"

"I don't know," he said. He paused in the library just long enough to let the hologram that hid the control center from the casual visitor recognize his retinal scan, and then ushered her in ahead of him. "But I intend to find out."

This room was a departure from the rest of the house, much more modern and without the artifacts and artworks that filled every nook and shelf outside. No concessions to the Luna Foundation were made in this space—the room was entirely given over to their true purpose here. It hummed with constant electrical energy; the computers never shut down; the lifeline of the house was never cut off.

At the moment, the room was going insane, humming with input. The many workstations were all on, their monitors showing a heavy gray fog snuggled up against every camera on the island. Bright explosions of color broke the grayness at odd patterns, leaving a brief instant of afterimage. But according to the sensors that accompanied the cameras, there was nothing there. No fog, no electricity, no changes in temperature, hot or cold. None of the usual signs of psychic phenomena. Absolutely nothing out of the ordinary, despite what the unblinking lenses of the security cameras were telling them.

"Then again, they didn't show David, either," Derek said under his breath. This system had not been his idea, and he didn't completely trust it. Not completely.

Grabbing a chair in front of the nearest terminal, Alex tuned the now-softly crying alarms out of her awareness and accessed the mainframe, her jaw falling open in disbelief.

"Derek, the P-waves, they're off the scale. Whatever's going on, it's all around us, blanketing the house. No, swamping it, like a tsunami." She tapped a few commands into the system, trying to get a better reading from psi-sensitive transistors, then looked up at her companion.

"It's trying to get in," he said, leaning over her to switch the display to the oversized screen set in the wall.

"What is?" she demanded, trying very hard not to let the rising hysteria she felt creep into her voice.

Derek kept staring at the screen, seeing something beyond the digital display. "Whatever it was that chased our young visitor to us, I suspect."

"You think David did this? That it's his fault?"

"His fault? No, perhaps not. But that it has to do with him, yes, that I believe. The timing is too close to be coincidental."

"Derek? Alex? What's going on?"

They turned to see Nick stumble into the room. Dressed hurriedly in jeans and a gray t-shirt, he was barefoot, but he was tucking a pistol into the back of his waistband, and his face was alert and awake.

"What the hell is going on?" he asked again, taking in the wildly-fluctuating screens and the alarm lights which still flickered redly. "It sounds like there's a hell of a storm going on outside, but it's clear, not a cloud in the sky. Full moon and all."

"You went outside?" Derek looked at him sharply, his body tensed, then relaxed marginally when Nick shook his head.

"Not with those alarms blaring. You think I'm crazy?"

He paused. "Okay, don't answer that. Just someone fill me in, okay? I'm about to wake you"—indicating Derek—"for your turn at babysitting, and all hell breaks loose. Don't worry, David's so out of it he didn't even twitch, and Rachel was going to check up on him in a bit, too. So. Anyone got a nice easy answer to what the hell's going on?"

"I am afraid not. We don't know the cause, either. Merely that there's a serious blast of psychic wind outside, trying to use us as a cat toy."

Nick looked at the screen again and did a double-take at the fog and colors swirling there.

"Clear, you said?" Derek asked.

Nick nodded, still staring, then he looked up at the ceiling as another heavy thump sounded against the roof overhead. Digging up a wry grin, he summed the entire situation in one sentence:

"This is going to be one of those days, isn't it?"

Within an hour, the thumping had settled down to a steady slap-wait-slap-wait, like the lash of a cat's tail as it waited outside a mousehole. And if the identity of the cat was still unknown, everyone knew who was playing the role of the mouse.

The fog and colors on the monitors intensified as the sun rose. With daybreak, both Alex and Derek could see the fog when they looked out the library's window, although Nick and Rachel both insisted that it was a clear, if overcast, dawn. By mid-morning, the entire building was coated in a heavy, dry fog unlike anything they had encountered before, even on a coast noted for its condensation.

They had cut the alarms, since everyone was up and alerted, and they now waited in an uneasy silence, punctuated by the rhythmic force outside.

Rachel, after double-checking Nick's assertion that

David had somehow slept through the uproar, had joined them in the office, bringing coffee and a plate of toasted and buttered bagels.

"I want everyone to eat something," she announced, placing the tray down on the table with a don't-argue-with-me clunk. She and Nick had taken their co-workers' words for it that the fog was there, but she still couldn't stop herself from double-checking the windows whenever she looked at the monitors.

"Facing the unknown on an empty stomach is not part of my battle plan," Nick reassured her, reaching around to lift a bagel off the top of the pile and biting into it with relish.

"Armageddon couldn't stop that man's stomach," Alex noted wryly from her position at the terminal, where she was still charting the P-waves.

Rachel smiled, prepping a mug of coffee and bringing it over to Derek, who was looking through several books spread out on the table in front of him. He looked up when she placed the steaming mug next to him, nodded his thanks, and went back to turning pages.

"I can't find a single reference that would match what is happening outside," he said in a tone of disgust.

Rachel picked up one of the books and studied the leather-bound cover. "Regions of Weather?" She flipped through the pages, and pursed her mouth in surprised interest. "Magical influences on weather patterns?"

"Acting under the logical assumption that someone— or something—has called these winds up and directed them against us, that seemed a good place to start. And since this fog, and the wind buffeting us, is clearly not of natural origin . . ."

"At least, not of natural direction," Alex clarified. "The winds themselves could be perfectly natural, re-directed here by the force showing up as P-waves."

Derek nodded, frowning thoughtfully. "Point taken."

"But if Alex is wrong? What if it's not just weird weather? Is it capable of real aggression?" Nick asked, swallowing the last bite of his breakfast and wiping buttery fingers on the back of his jeans.

"What do you mean?" Rachel asked, placing the book back down on the table.

"Just that with all our sensors and readouts and sticking our heads out the window, we haven't tested the one really important thing: can whatever's outside hurt us?"

"Nick, I don't think that's such a wise idea," Derek began, but the younger man cut him off.

"I know, and I don't want to go out there either. But sitting in here waiting is starting to wear on my nerves."

Derek looked at him, then nodded once, in resigned agreement.

"Derek, Nick, you can't be serious," Rachel protested. "It would be insanity to go out into that without knowing what it is or who sent it."

"We know that it hasn't tried to get past the wards yet," Derek replied, referring to the magical sigils carved and painted into the house itself when it was built.

"That could just mean that it can't," Alex observed. Then, more slowly, she added, "or that they know they can't get in, and so aren't even trying."

"Which would suggest that it's got some serious knowledge of our defenses, which is not a welcome thought. But even so, to not even make the attempt? That seems very odd. And indicative of something other than a completely hostile intent. All right, Nick. But be careful."

The ex-SEAL quirked the corner of his mouth up in a grin. "My middle name," he replied, leaving the office with a purpose to his stride.

"Yes, but his first name is too often "Not," Derek said, standing to follow. "Rachel, Alex? I suspect we should be on hand, as witnesses, if nothing else."

"You go on," Alex said. "I want to keep an eye on the monitors. See if there's any spike or letdown when Nick does whatever he's going to do."

"Agreed."

"Derek?" Rachel asked almost too nonchalantly.

"Hmmm?" He looked sideways down at her as they walked.

"Did you notice, back in the Control Room? How quickly we went from talking about weather, to talking about something . . ."

"Something living?"

"Yes."

"Yes, I had noticed that."

She pursed her mouth thoughtfully. "Just thought I'd mention it."

It was easier, somehow, to slip into the assumption that it was supernatural rather than natural. The supernatural was easier to fight in some ways. Storms, whether natural or somehow induced, were devastating in a way that couldn't be defended against. Someone— or something—that could control the weather . . .

I'd rather face the devil himself than Mother Nature, Rachel thought. *At least there's a record of people outwitting him . . .*

They caught up with Nick by the front door before Rachel could drag more out of Derek. The younger man turned to look over his shoulder at them, an uneasy grin on his face. "Maybe you should have a rope ready to tie around my waist?"

Derek held up a length of coiled hemp he had picked up from a closet along the way. "Ahead of you on that."

"Great. But be careful, okay? I don't want to have to explain to my next date why I've got a nasty case of rope burn."

"I'm sure you could think of something that would

57

pass muster," Derek said dryly, tying the rope around Nick's waist.

That done, they looked around for something to attach the other end to. But everything they saw was either too lightweight, too fragile, or too expensive to risk. Finally, they settled on the bannister. The rope was just long enough to let him step out through the doorway and onto the wide stone patio out front.

Rachel double-checked the knots, then looked up and nodded.

"As ready as we're going to be."

Derek turned to Nick, who shook off the older man's concerns. "I'm not going to do anything stupid," he said. "Just open the door, stick my head out, and see what there is to see. No heroics, no sudden moves."

"Who are you, and what have you done with Nick Boyle?" Rachel asked with a faint smile.

"Funny." Without further ado, Nick tugged once at the rope and then threw open the heavy door to the outside.

And Derek, his Sight showing him what others missed, *saw* the fog reach out, saw it curl around the younger man—

and throw him back into the house.

Nick landed with a heavy thud, sliding back several feet on the wooden floor and ending up at Rachel's feet by the stairs. He shook his head roughly. "Whoa. I guess we're not supposed to go outside, huh?"

"House arrest," Rachel said, reaching down to help the shaken young man to his feet.

"But why?" Nick asked, after checking to make sure that everything was still in one piece and where it was supposed to be. "And what? Because I'll tell you, anything that could toss me like that . . ." Nick let his voice trail off. Whatever it was that was out there, he knew for a fact that it hadn't raised a sweat in tossing him around. Just "wham, slam, thank you sucker."

"I think that we should be asking that question of our house guest," Derek said, crossing the foyer to close the door against a wall of gray mist that still filled the open space. "Whatever this is, I am convinced that it has to do with him and his appearance here."

"But if he doesn't remember . . ."

"He will." And there was a wealth of grim promise in those words.

The alarms had been designed to not sound quite as loudly in the area referred to as the "guest wing" in an effort to shield visitors from the chaos that often seemed part and parcel of membership in the Legacy. When Rachel stuck her head into the room they had settled David into, he was a lump under the pillows, apparently undisturbed by the thumping of the wind against the walls and roof. Stripes of gray shadow and darkness painted the interior, washing out the normally cheerful blue and cream decor and making it seem ominous rather than warm. Despite herself, Rachel had shuddered, chalking it up to the early morning hour, and the terrible wind raging outside.

"David?"

No answer, only the soft sound of breathing and the steady rise and fall of the covers. He had managed to take half a bowl of soup, according to Nick, but then slid back into a healing sleep that, it would seem, still held him in its embrace.

Satisfied, she had closed the door softly. The sound of her footsteps clicked down the hallway, then faded into silence.

A moment passed. Then another.

The body under the covers shifted, then sat up. A wave of dizziness seemed to strike him, and he reached out to steady himself on the brass headrest.

The feel of the cool metal on his skin did the trick, and he was able to get out of bed without further incident. He was clad only in a pair of white boxers, from a pile of clothing Rachel had left for him, and his skin was as pale as the faint light now coming in through the window.

He had dreamed as he slept. Dreams that made him twist against waking, like a swimmer unsure which direction is the surface, and air. Dreams that left him more wearied when he woke than before he had slept.

A sudden thump and slide of wind against the roof made him startle like a deer, freezing in position as though the lack of movement would render him invisible to predators. He swallowed convulsively, his frame trembling from the strain of standing upright. He knew. He knew what was out there.

The windowpane rattled, as though something outside were trying to reach in, and he half-lunged, half-fell across the room to where his clothing was carefully hung across the back of a straight-back chair. The material was still damp, and from that he gauged the passage of time. No more than a day, perhaps only half that. There was still time. If he hurried . . .

Digging into the folds, he came up triumphantly with a small leather pouch tied with a thong.

His legs gave out on him then, half in relief, half in exhaustion, and he collapsed onto the chair. Pulling open the pouch, he reached in and extracted something clenched tightly in his hand. He stared at his fist, as though gauging what he was about to do, then stood up and walked to the outside wall, carefully skirting the window. Dangerous. So dangerous . . .

Opening his fist slightly, he tilted his hand and let a faint, fine shower of something that caught what little light was creeping into the room and shimmered as it fell to the floor. He moved in baby steps, making sure that the debris fell in a steady stream, leaving a narrow trail on the floor just along the wall. The metal shavings glinted against the hardwood floor, and he was thankful that he had taken the time to scrape them bit by painful bit from the few pieces of scrap he could scrounge during his captivity.

Cold iron. Every story said it was proof against the supernatural. Against attack—or influence. Through man-worked metals They couldn't reach him. If only this house were newer, a skyscraper or something made of a more hostile fabric than wood and stone . . .

The wind seemed to know what he was doing, rising in intensity, and slamming into the house just a step ahead of him. The first time he jumped, and his hand jerked, causing the line to quaver.

"Damn," he muttered, nudging the mess into an unbroken line with the side of his bare foot.

After that, his hand remained steady, even though his face showed the strain he was under, both mentally and physically. The filings clung to his palm and had to be brushed off to fall correctly.

When he was finished, he let his arms fall to his sides, quivering. His skin was coated with cold sweat and looked the color and consistency of old cottage cheese. But the wind's assaults on the window and roof faded and disappeared, although he could still feel them trying to reach in through other parts of the house.

He didn't think it would hold them forever. But maybe, just maybe, it would be long enough.

Long enough for what, he wasn't certain. To sift though his memories. To make sure of his new allies. To decide what he would do with the rest of his life. But for now, it was enough that he was free. He was safe.

When his limbs felt strong enough, he pushed off from the chair and shuffled back to the bed, crawling in and pulling the covers securely around him with a palpable sense of relief. And despite the anxiety which still clung to him, he was truly asleep within minutes.

Outside, the wind raged and screamed impotently. And below the window, the silent fog pried slender fingers into the mortar and stone facade.

FIVE

The Control Room was beginning to take on the aspects of battle headquarters. Which it was, in fact, if a battle in which no shots had been fired, no overt hostilities exchanged.

Only the strange gray fog holding them under house arrest.

Once the shock of Nick's experiment had worn off, Derek had put Security Plan B into motion, which mainly involved getting noncombatants out of the line of fire. They had a small staff in during the day, but most of them left at night for their own homes. If they tried to come back today, the fog would undoubtedly turn them back.

Gently, Nick hoped.

He checked the log to see who was heading up the handful of support staff remaining on the island. A team of fifteen, working twelve-hour rotations out of the small building which handled the Luna Foundation's obvious security system. Set on a cliff looking out toward the wide expanses of the Pacific, they were connected to the rest of the island only by a wide dirt track that was completely impassable in this fog.

"Even assuming we could get out of the house," he muttered, holding the phone to his ear and waiting for someone to pick up the intra-island line at the other end.

"Georges? It's Nick. Is everyone okay out there?"

A long pause while the other voice spoke. Nick's brow furrowed, and he cast a worried glance at the others in the room.

"Nothing? No weird weather, no—huh? Yeah, people getting "wiggies" qualifies. Okay, look, we've got a possible situation here. Yeah, possible. No incoming yet. Pack up your stuff, put the equipment on automatic, and get the hell out of there, okay?"

He paused, as though waiting for an argument. Fortunately, anyone who worked for the Luna Foundation learned to react first and ask awkward questions later. Especially if they worked the security detail. He said his farewells, then pushed a button to change to an outside line.

"Do you think that they will be all right?" Rachael asked Derek, her voice low and worried.

"They should be fine, so long as they stay away from the house itself," he replied, looking up in time to see Nick hang up the phone and rejoin them. "As I said before, I don't believe that the force outside, whatever it may be, means to harm us. At least, not without provocation."

"Yeah, right," Nick muttered, rubbing the portion of his anatomy that had taken the brunt of his experiment. "Define 'harm,' willya?"

"That was merely a warning," Derek said. "I think."

"That's comforting," Nick said, pulling the comfy chair over with effort and settling himself gingerly.

"And what about the fact that the main phone line's down?"

"What?" Alex turned in her chair and reached automatically not for the phone, but to access the modem connection. Seconds ticked off, and a small "no dial tone" logo appeared in the middle of the nearest screen.

A small whimper rose from the back of her throat, and even in his discomfort Nick spared a smirk for her. "Addiction is an ugly thing, Alex. Think of this as Internet intervention."

"Hah. Funny."

Rachel reached for her cell phone, turning it on and hitting a button. She held it to her ear, frowned, and hit the button again. "Nothing. No dial tone. And . . . Kat. Oh god, if Kat tries to call—"

"She will assume we had line difficulty," Derek reassured her. "Nothing out of the ordinary. The phone company won't send anyone out for a day or so, based on our past history of brownouts and downed lines. They—whatever "they" are—have cut us off for the duration, but I suspect that was all they intended."

"Because we have something it—they—want," Alex said, one eye on the monitor charting the intensity of the winds outside but her attention focused on the conversation at hand.

"Yes. David." The Precept of the Legacy House frowned briefly, clearly not relishing the coming confrontation with their house guest, who was currently under discrete lock and key.

"We don't know that," Nick protested.

"No, we don't. But his arrival was followed too quickly by this fog for us to assume coincidence. Alex, was the camera in David's room set to record?"

"Oh. No." She blinked, as though surprised at her lapse. Normally, the internal camera system was turned off in the bedrooms, as much to save tape as to ensure privacy. She flicked a switch on the control board and entered the code for that particular room's camera to turn itself on and begin recording. Setting one monitor to display, Alex put the now-running camera on-line. The live view, although grainy, clearly showed him lying quietly in bed with a paperback book on his lap.

He was awake but had apparently made no attempt to get out of bed again, much less leave the room. He merely lay there, taking a sip of water every now and again, almost too obviously not looking out the windows.

Curious, but not incriminating. The lack of interest might prove that he knew what was out there, and why. Or it might be that he simply wasn't aware of anything outside his own situation. The mind tends to skip right over evidence of the paranormal, especially when it could be discredited as a normal-looking phenomenon, such as fog on the coast of San Francisco.

"In the meantime," Derek continued, looking away from the display with an effort, "We need to beef up some of our security measures. It may be that this force cannot enter the house, or it may be that it simply does not feel the need for such a step. But we cannot take either assumption for granted."

"You're talking about whatever it is like it's a living creature again," Rachel pointed out, then raised her hands in surrender as the other three looked at her with identical expressions. "Okay, no more psychoanalyzing."

Derek nodded, acknowledging both her promise and the underlying concerns, then turned to look at Nick. The ex-SEAL had been shifting uncomfortably in his chair, fiddling with the extra small throw pillow Rachel had tossed him to cushion his posterior some more. While normally the sight would have made the older man smile, the gravity of the situation kept him from reacting to the sight of the tough young fighter squirming like a schoolboy who had been paddled.

"Nick, I want you to go over the security measures once again. Make certain that there have been no breaches, no breakdowns in the electrical system. Divert power to the alarms, and make sure that the back-up system is enabled. I don't want to be caught with our pants down if it—they, whatever—try to cut the power."

Nick stood thankfully, wincing as his other muscles protested.

"And take some aspirin while you're up," Derek added, unable to resist. "I'm the only one allowed to have back pain like that around here."

Alex hid a grin at Nick's growl as he limped with dramatic emphasis out of the room. "And I suppose you want me to walk the Line?" she asked, referring to the Legacy's secondary line of slightly more esoteric defenses.

In addition to the sigils and wardings built into the house at its construction, the Line was a psychic thread sewn into the interior walls, fine-tuned so that any mental vibration would alert sensitives within. "Walking it" involved having a sensitive trace the fibers of that thread, ensuring that none of them had been tampered with. Boring work, but no worse than what Derek had Nick redoing for the third time in twelve hours.

And that thought made her wonder about something.

"Derek, this morning, the silence that woke me up—could that have been a reaction from the Line? Could whatever's out there have been probing us?"

"If so," the Legacy's other sensitive replied, "the fact that the Line did not go off then would indicate that it was a probe more delicate that any we have on record."

"But it is possible?" Rachel asked, coming alert.

"Yes. It is possible."

Rachel shivered delicately. Although her work with

the Legacy had brought her into contact with ghosts, demons, and every other possible manifestation of the supernatural, the idea of mental manipulation still left her feeling uneasy.

Alex could sympathize. It gave her the willies, too.

"In the meantime, Rachel, why don't you bring our guest downstairs to the library. I would feel better if we were able to keep a more immediate eye on him and not rely upon mechanicals."

"Don't let Nick hear you dis his camera network," Alex warned as she got up to leave the room. He had spent an entire week setting the system up, a week of intense work and much fluent cursing, requiring electricians to come in afterwards and repair his wiring job.

"Do you think that the phones being out will cause a problem?" Rachel asked as Derek took the seat Alex had vacated and pulled a keyboard toward him.

"I have already let the other Houses know what is going on," he replied. "If something should happen, I want a full report to go to others, just in case this isn't an isolated incident."

She glanced at the monitor displaying David's prone form almost involuntarily. "I thought you said that this was centered around David?"

"I suspect it is, yes. But I'm not willing to risk the rest of the Legacy on that assumption."

Rachel stood, then paused by his chair, resting one hand lightly on his shoulder. "Thank you," she said.

"For what?"

"For not saying 'I told you so' about bringing in another stray."

"We exist to protect the innocent," he reminded her. "And, until proven otherwise, we must assume that David is indeed innocent and in need of that protection."

Left alone in the Control Center, Derek ran his hand through his shaggy, graying hair, wondering if his words had convinced her that she was not to blame. Probably not. Rachel had an awesome ability to assume responsibility. Perhaps it came with being a mother. Derek stopped and smiled reluctantly. Perhaps it came with being a member of the Legacy.

He cast one last look at the wall screen that still displayed the P-wave activity and shook his head. While the others were using technology and the psychic arts to research the problem, he would use more old-fashioned, pedantic means.

"When in doubt," he lectured the empty room, "hit the books."

Rachel climbed the stairs, her hand running along the bannister absently, so familiar with her surroundings that she barely looked at them. Part of her mind was on Katherine, of course. But the larger percentage was focused on the young man in the room upstairs. The team was so close-knit, their individual quirks forgiven even as they occasionally annoyed, that it was interesting to see the different reactions to a stranger. And from someone's reactions, she had discovered, you could intuit a great deal about the person being reacted to.

Take her own emotions, for example. Nick teased her about thinking that she was the mother of all things, and that all things should wear a sweater, but her mom-sense had kicked into overdrive the moment she saw David hanging limp in Jonathan's arms.

Something's wrong with that guy, her instinct had whispered to her. *Something you can't fix*. She wanted that voice to be wrong. But somehow, she suspected that it wasn't.

Her feet stopped without prompting from her brain, and she realized that she had arrived at her destination. Taking a deep breath, she cleared her mind of doubts and pushed open the bedroom door.

"Hi there. Feel like blowing this bird cage?"

David's winning grin was answer enough and gave her another twinge of guilt. He was obviously starved for human contact, and they had all been too busy to spend time with him up here. So Derek had unwillingly given his permission for Rachel to escort him within the main wing. If nothing else, it would keep him under surveillance better than the camera could. And the wardings were stronger in the main wing as well, should whatever was directing the fog make a direct assault.

"Okay, then." Rachel dropped a fresh pile of clothing—pilfered from Nick's closet—on the chair and turned to her charge. "Let's get you into something a little more suited for wandering around this drafty barn."

"I can dress myself," he protested, getting out of bed. But after a full day of enforced bed rest, he was still more than a little shaky on his feet. He swayed once, reached out to support himself on the footboard of the bed, and his grin turned apologetic. "But maybe you could just stand by and keep me company?"

Rachel ended up doing more than that, holding him upright as he put a pair of sweatpants and a shirt on over the boxers that he had already borrowed. The sweats were a little short, the worn elastic bagging around his calves, but the shirt hung loose from shoulders leaner than the original owner's.

"Will Nick mind that I have taken his clothing?"

"What? Oh, no, don't worry about it. He'll just blame Alex, if anybody. She's forever borrowing his stuff and forgetting to tell him. Why, I remember one time, she took his brand new ski jacket because hers had gotten wet in the rain, and he spent half an hour racing about this place, trying to remember where he had left it."

With her chatter giving him something other than his weakness to focus on, they moved slowly into the hallway. His bare feet, a full size smaller than Nick's but much wider, and therefore unshoeable, made an odd, soft slapping noise on the wooden floor, compared to the tapping of her crepe-soled shoes.

Once through the bedroom door, he moved away from her support, apparently intent on getting downstairs under his own steam. Mindful of young male pride, she stepped back to allow him that much independence. But as her story rambled from purloined ski jackets to other embarrassing stories about Nick and Alex, she kept a careful eye on his progress, alert to any weakness or disorientation.

They made it all the way down the guest wing's hallway without incident. But when he reached the narrow carpeted runner that was laid in the wider main hall, he stumbled slightly, his toe catching on the rough-textured edging.

"Do you need some help?" she asked, stepping to his side, her hand outstretched to keep him from falling into a small hardwood table holding a tasteful and disgustingly expensive lamp.

"No, thank you. I can manage on my own." His voice was tight, almost angry, as though losing his balance was a sin, a shameful thing.

"All right. If you need any help, I'll be right here." And she stepped back half a pace, letting him shuffle down the hallway toward the main stairs.

Once there, he leaned on the banister for a moment, seemingly to regather his strength. Recovered slightly, he looked up and saw out the huge plate glass window in the hallway that looked out toward the mainland.

He started, although that view was still clear, looking back hesitantly over his shoulder at Rachel. His face, before knotted in pain and concentration, was now sheened over with fear.

"What do you see?" she asked gently.

"Nothing. N-nothing."

She should have just let it alone. He was clearly not recovered yet, and badgering a patient while moving him downstairs was not on the AMA's approved medical practices list. But this wasn't on one of the AMA's traditional patient/physician situations, either, and that changed the rules a little.

Something's wrong with him. Something you can't fix.
Trying to keep her voice calm, she asked the obvious, unavoidable question. "You can see what's out there, can't you, David?"

And then he did lose his balance, almost pitching headfirst down the stairs.

"Damn," she said, racing to catch him around the waist. His body was lighter than she recalled from their earlier encounters, as though his bones had been hollowed out, and the skin she touched was drier, more papery.

"You okay? Come on, now. Don't look at the window, look away. Let's take this one step at a time, shall we?"

He nodded, this time allowing her to support him as they moved down the steps. Obviously trying to keep from thinking about what he had seen, David stared straight ahead, barely blinking. His body was stiff, like a monster-movie zombie, and Rachel thought seriously about turning him around and marching him back up to bed.

But slowly, to her great relief, as they descended the stairs, he roused slightly, his attention caught by first one detail of the house, then another. Blinking, gaping a little like a backwoods rube, he stopped with both feet on a wide carpeted step, finally taking in his surroundings. Rachel noticed his slightly awed expression, and laughed softly. "I suppose it is a little overwhelming at first. But after a while, you honestly don't notice it any more."

David took a few more steps then stopped again, staring at a small statue set in a niche in the wall. She followed his stare and let out a sharp exhalation, half amused, half resigned. "Okay. Maybe you don't get used to all of it." She tugged gently on his arm. "Come on. You don't want to stare at that too long. I can't imagine why Derek keeps it out in plain sight like that."

They made it to the library without further incident. Steering David to the nearest chair, Rachel stepped back and studied her patient critically. His color was still bad, although nothing a few weeks in the tropics couldn't cure. But he was too winded from what should have been a simple walk downstairs. It had been twenty-four hours. Even assuming he had used every scrape of energy however he arrived here, he should have recovered more than this by now.

An ugly suspicion crept into her brain, and she shook it away. The tests had come back negative.

"How do you feel?"

"Tired," he admitted. "Like I swam a marathon."

"You did, actually," she reminded him and got a pleasant, if tired, grin in return.

"Yeah, I guess I did, didn't I?"

"So you remember that much, at least."

Derek's voice, breaking into their conversation, surprised them both. Rachel, who knew that he had stepped back into the library through the hologram wall, recovered more swiftly than David, who gaped at the man who had seemingly appeared out of thin air.

"Derek, right?" He covered his surprise with bravado that didn't quite come off right. "You own this place."

"In a manner of speaking, yes." Derek moved around them, circling as though studying his prey. Rachel, who knew his methods, still couldn't help being unnerved. With his brooding countenance and direct gaze, Derek

Rayne was an imposing predator when he chose to be. Even without a sin on your soul, you felt the need to confess.

David, however, must have been as pure as a newborn babe, for he met Derek's gaze with a clear, steady regard. All the uncertainty and hesitations of before were gone, leaving behind a blandly innocent face, clear, trusting brown eyes set over that unfortunate nose.

"Thank you for taking me in. I don't know what would have happened to me if they had caught me, but I don't think I would have liked it." He smiled, that sweet quirk of a grin, then let it fade into an uncertain frown.

"You will let me stay, won't you? You'll protect me?"

Rachel looked to Derek, holding down firmly on her instinctive "of course we will." This was Legacy business now, and in the final analysis, that made it Derek's call. But still, how could he not grant sanctuary? Whatever was out there had clearly shown itself to be unfriendly.

Derek crouched in front of David's chair, placing his hands on the armrests and staring up at the younger man, one intent gaze meeting the other.

"We have opened our doors to you, made you welcome, and protected you, all without question. But what you're asking now is more than a roof to shelter you, or food and clothing. It would require that we place our own lives in jeopardy; to die, if need be, to keep you from harm. If we grant you sanctuary within this House," and the capital H was almost visible in his words, "then you owe us something as well. Such as the truth."

David started to speak, glib reassurances falling off his lips, and Derek held up one hand to stop him.

"The truth, David. Everything that you can remember. We know that what follows you is not a gang, as you claimed. It is not human. What is it? What have you done to so enrage a supernatural force?"

David started back in surprise, hitting the unyielding chair back with his shoulders. His gaze, now panicky beyond what could be considered normal, darting from Derek to Rachel and back again. But neither Legacy member gave ground. Derek was granite, Rachel an only slightly warmer stone. She hated to do it, but if this was the route Derek was taking, then she would not contradict him. Not in public, anyway. Not in front of an outsider.

Finally, the young man exhaled, and relaxed forward a little, his shoulders slumping. At this sign of capitulation, Derek moved away, pulling a chair from the table behind him and sitting in it, still close enough to David to touch him, but allowing some breathing space, to give the impression of freedom. Rachel allowed herself a slight smile at that, since it was the direct result of a prolonged argument between the two of them months earlier about personal space and the abuse thereof. Who said you couldn't teach an old dog new tricks?

"They are a gang," David said, studying the weave of the sweatpants across his knee intently. "Everything I told you was true, everything I can remember. I was running from them, trying to escape through trees, through this fog and haze, and I could hear them behind me. And I knew I had to get away, or they would kill me for sure this time."

"This time? You had tried to escape before?"

David hesitated, looking up to meet Rachel's concerned gaze. "I . . . all I remember was this pain in my veins, like fire. Screaming until my throat was raw, and the feel of chains . . ."

David held up his arms, seemingly surprised when there were no marks on his wrists. "I remember being bound, tied down. Heavy chains, catching light, reflecting back into my eyes until I cried. I couldn't see anything, and then I couldn't feel anything . . . and the rest, the rest I don't remember."

Derek looked up at Rachel as well, who shrugged her shoulders. His pain seemed genuine, his fear was unmistakably real—but something was triggering Derek's unease, and she had nothing to counter it with. Other than the fact that they had a young man asking them for aid against a supernatural force that had demonstrated a less-than-caring concern for him.

That should be enough. Shouldn't it?

"I have an idea," she said, looking for something to break the stalemate. "David, how do you feel about hypnosis?"

"Hypnosis? Like a trance?" Something inside those brown eyes flickered, and he shook his head violently, his hair whipping around his face in abject denial. "No. Nothing like that. I don't like not being in control any more."

Derek moved away to let Rachel move in, her expertise taking precedence in this situation. Her voice took on the distanced-yet-caring tone she used in practice. "No trance, no. It's nothing at all like you see in the movies, or hear jokes about. I promise. The hypnosis is merely a way to allow your mind to calm down, to relax. Once you're ready, we should be able to get beyond the barriers in your memory. But you will remain aware of your surroundings to a certain extent, and I won't be able to push you anywhere you're not ready to go."

David looked ready to bolt, despite her reassurances.

"I think this falls under the 'no secrets' agreement. We need to know what is facing us," Derek reminded them, his voice rough with encroaching exhaustion, and Rachel wondered briefly how much sleep he had gotten before this all began, knowing he would get none until it was over.

"And if hypnosis is what it takes," he continued, "then I suggest that we get started."

In other words, Rachel thought, put up or get out. But she couldn't bring herself to be angry at Derek. Not when the safety of everyone on the island might be at risk. In fact, considering Derek's occasional temper, he was being quite well behaved.

"So?" she asked David, raising one blond eyebrow in an expression that was at once amused and compassionate, what Alex called her trust-me-I'm-a-doctor face. And, as usual, it worked.

"You promise that you won't make me quack like a duck or anything?" David relented.

Rachel laughed. "I promise. No ducks. You'll be in control of yourself. All I'll be doing is leading you into areas that might otherwise remain closed off to your conscious mind."

He considered that for a long moment. "Then . . . okay. What do I have to do?"

"It's quite simple, really." Rachel pulled up a chair and sat down next to him. "First, I want you to relax. Just let your arms hang by your side, hands in your lap. That's good. Now close your eyes and breathe slowly. That's it. Breathe in, breathe out. Good. Feel the rise and fall of your chest, and concentrate on that."

She waited a few moments until he was completely focused on his breathing. "Good, very good. Now I want you to visualize ten fingers, all right? Ten fingers, held in front of you. Nod your head when you can see them in front of you."

She waited for the slight dip of his head to indicate his readiness.

"Good. Now I want you to begin to count backward from ten, slowly, and at each count one finger will bend down, folding back into the palm. Right, like that, now let's begin with ten."

"Ten," he echoed, one of his own fingers folding over in reaction to his mental picture. "Nine." A pause. "Eight."

"Breathe, remember to breathe deeply and—"

"Seven." A deep breath, and his shoulders lost their tension. "Six." That finger barely twitched. "Five." Breath. "Four." His voice became fainter, barely a mumble. "Three." His hands melted against his thighs, no longer reacting to the countdown. "Two."

Once the number one had been reached, his lips moving but the actual word inaudible, he was a model subject; relaxed but attentive, following her suggestions without hesitation or resistance. Five minutes after they began, Rachel judged him ready to begin remembering.

"David, can you still hear me?"

"Mmmmhhhmmmm."

"Good. I want you to think back, okay? Think back to last week. Think back to what you were doing, where you were."

There was the slightest strain of his body, nothing obvious, but Rachel noted the signs of resistance immediately.

"It's all right. Everything you see, everything you hear, everything you feel, it is all at a distance. Nothing there hurts you. Now. Look around, David. Where are you? What do you see?"

David's eyes opened. The brown orbs stared past her, past Derek, out of the library and into someplace else. "Fog. Always fog. Never anything but fog until I think I've lost my mind. I would kill to see the sun again. I would die to see the sun again."

Rachel squelched the immediate irreverent thought— he was in Vancouver?—and tried to prod him forward slightly. "What is around you? Look down, David. What do you see?"

He responded to her voice, moving his head down to

stare at his wrists. "Chains. They've chained me again. For my own good, they say. To keep me from hurting myself again." His voice was bitter, his mouth twisting harshly, making him seem years older. Now that the barrier had been breached, he seemed desperate to get it all out, the words tumbling over each other.

"They say they love me, that they only want to keep me well, but they're killing me. Every single day that passes, they take more out of me, they leave me hollow like themselves. Like these," and he lifted his hands slightly, as though to show them the chains.

Derek, following the motion of the younger man's hands, started slightly. Rachel managed to spare just enough attention from David to query the older man.

"A vision," he said softly, breathing as though slightly winded. "The chains about his wrists. Silver filigree, as a bracelet. Light and delicate, and as implacable as forged steel. They glowed with power, Rachel. A power that should be familiar, feels like something I have encountered before, and yet it is nothing I have ever felt before."

Rachel turned her attention back to David, waiting for Derek to catch his breath from the intensity of his Sight. She knew better than to offer him support, or even acknowledge that he was having any difficulty.

Finally, Derek regained enough control to finish his comments. "Whatever it is, wherever this force comes from or whatever powers it, it is very strong. Like braided strands of power, subtle, but unbreakable. And angry. Very, very angry. That must be what Alex was picking up on, what she meant by bad vibes."

"But why? And how? And, more to the point, who?"

"Only he can tell us that," Derek responded.

Rachel nodded, picking up the threads of the session again. "What else, David? What else do you see? Is there anyone near you?"

"Chais. And Mirlac." He said their names oddly, as though sounding something out in a difficult language. His voice hovered between fear and fascination, and Rachel frowned. He seemed to be under far deeper than she could account for. She shrugged, mentally. Some people were more susceptible to hypnotic suggestion than others. It was an unexpected bonus.

"Who are they? Who are Chais and Mir—"

"Mirlac. My . . . guards. They're always there. Always waiting, watching. Hungry. So beautiful, so deadly. . . . but not like her. Nothing is like her . . ."

Rachel cast another quick look at Derek for instructions, but he seemed as captivated as David by what they saw.

"Wonderful," she muttered to herself. "David, who are they? Who are these people who are watching you?"

"Not people," he responded dreamily, still hung between warring emotions, lost to all awareness of anything other than his opening memories. "She."

"She?" Rachel puzzled at that, realization coming on the heels of Derek's gasp. *"Sidhe," he said. Sidhe.* Of all the strangeness she had encountered in her time with the Legacy, with ghosts and demons and supernatural creatures formed by curses and hatred, somehow she had never considered this. And the part of her that still thought in terms of pastel watercolors of laughing sprites, Shakespeare's sanitized Puck and Tolkien's elves, was overpowered by the part of her that knew the Brothers Grimm were probably understating the matter.

Elves. From all stories, they were dark, powerful, changeable creatures. Even if David named them only from his own perceptions . . . even the most amiable of otherworldly beings were dangerous to cross.

Unless, of course, his mind had merely broken. Unless his abuse had been at the hands of humans; a mortal evil so unbearable that he created these phantasms to cover it in more acceptable disguise . . .

And then how do you explain the mist, Rachel? Or the thump-a-thump on the roof this morning? Or Nick's little trick in the doorway?

"But you escaped," she said out loud, hoping to get him—them both—away from the fascination even the memory of those creatures seemed to hold.

"Yes." The pride in his voice now was unmistakable. "They became careless. I lulled them. Let them believe I had accepted my fate. Pretended to accept their touches, their pettings like some toothless dog. And once I acted the part of the obedient toy, they let me slip my leash. I was given freedom to roam the woods, with only the hounds to follow and keep me close."

Rachel kept her gaze on David's face. What he was saying was of less interest to her right now than why he was saying it. He was far too deeply under right now for her comfort. It was almost as though he had been preprogrammed to slip into deep hypnosis at the slightest suggestion.

He might have been brainwashed by his captors. A combination of sleep deprivation, hunger, and phsyical coercion.

Or magic. The Sidhe were supposed to use glamour on their victims, which was a type of hypnosis, wasn't it? Oh, for a textbook on things like this!

She pulled her attention back to David with an effort, aware that he was still speaking.

"They were cautious. Canny. But I waited, and watched, and one day I saw the break in the fog they use to keep their lands safe. I slipped through, sideways and sly, and lost the hounds behind me. I wasn't thinking of escape, so they couldn't read it in me. But I did it. I ran until I thought my lungs would burst, through stinging briars and grabbing willow trees, got out of the fog and could feel the sunlight on my skin even through the rain."

A pause, and he shuddered; even deep hypnosis was not enough to keep the fear completely at bay. "But they found me again. Found me, chased me. And now they're here. And they want me back. I won't go back. I won't! I won't go back!"

His voice escalated to shouts, and Rachel had no option but to bring him back into awareness quickly, before he injured himself. But he was panicking, floundering like a swimmer caught in the undertow of his own memories, and she couldn't reach him.

"Derek, help me!" she said, breaking Derek from his own Sight-trance enough to help her hold the young man down as he thrashed in his chair, trying to escape once again.

Between the two of them, they were able to break through to David and calm him back into semicoherence. A towel to dry the sweat along his neck and back was procured from the nearest bathroom, and a mug of lukewarm coffee poured from the thermos Rachel had brought with her that morning was placed in his hands, then they left him alone with his thoughts. Standing a distance across the library—close enough to react should he need them, but far enough for privacy on both sides—the two Legacy members combined their impressions of the hypnosis session.

"Well, that was interesting." A look out the window reminded her that mundane reasons were pretty much dead in the water at this point. She told Derek her theory of glamour abuse, for lack of a better term, and he agreed that it was probably a valid explanation. But that still left several very important questions unanswered.

"The trauma of escaping seems to have caused his amnesia. But why? All recorded cases indicate that returning to the mortal world after a stay with the Sidhe causes memory to *return*, not disappear. Could it be that the trauma of breaking free, breaking through from one world to the next, might have caused his brain to short out, for lack of a better term?"

Rachel blew the hair out of her eyes in exasperation. "It could be. I suppose. Damnit, Derek, this wasn't exactly covered in medical school!"

"Yes, I know. I'm sorry. But you agree that it is plausible?

"Plausible, yes. Not knowing what the nature of the barrier is, or how he managed to break through, or what his state was on the other side, anything is plausible at this point." She was aware that her voice was rising and took pains to tamp down the emotions behind it. She was frustrated, Derek was frustrated, and certainly David was frustrated. But losing it now wouldn't help anyone.

"All right. Plausible, but not confirmed. Next question—how did he escape? If the Sidhe have indeed been holding him captive, it is quite astonishing that he escaped, especially on his own. Typically, such an escape requires the aid of another."

"Like Thomas the Rhymer?" Glad of another avenue of thought, Rachel began to pace, trying to remember what she could of that story.

"Exactly. That legend says that his ladylove caught at him as the Sidhe rode by her, held on despite the magic they used, and that alone won him away."

"Her steadfast heart." Rachel's voice was wistful, remembering the ghost she had once helped find his own way back to those he had loved in life.

"True love has always been known to be a factor in relations with the faerie kingdom," Derek agreed. "And in our own experiences with the supernatural as well."

"But that isn't the case here," Rachel said, bringing them back to the original question. "No true love waiting for him, or he would be with her. Or him, not to be politically incorrect. So, how did he escape?"

"More to the point," Derek said, looking at the wall monitor, "is how do we keep him away from them now that they're all here?"

To that, she had no answer, falling into a bemused silence as her brain tried to wrap itself around everything they had just learned.

"Hey guys!" Alex breezed in through the open doorway. She had obviously taken time to stop at her room and shower before returning and was now dressed in jeans and a worn, blue sweater.

"Fog's starting to settle in but good, even Nick can see it now a little. We've got some resonance on the Line, look's like someone plucked at it, but no breaches anywhere. So we're in the clear there—" She stopped, looking at the two of them, and then at David still shivering over his coffee. "Whoops. What happened?"

S I X

"Faeries." Nick exhaled loudly though his nose. "You know, I didn't like them when my mom read me those old stories, I didn't like them when they were tall pale pointy-eared guys with swords who sang all the time, and I don't like them when they're overly aggressive fog. And I really don't like them when they start abducting guys off the street as play toys."

"You don't know that's how he ended up in Faerie," Rachel protested.

"What, you think he got snatched out of a cradle somewhere? Come on, Rach . . ."

They had taken up their usual positions around the long table in the library that Alex called the Brainstorming Table, sharing the results of the day's investigations. Rachel and Derek had just filled the other two members of the team in on the results of the hypnosis session with David, and what little they had managed to glean from that. Alex, frowning thoughtfully, had nodded. It made sense with what she had been able to pick up from Walking the Line, and the sensations which had woken her that morning.

Nick, however, was less sanguine. Apparently, demons, ghosts and vampires, among others, were easier for him to accept than what Alex insisted on referring to as the Fey Folk. Something about the conflicting stories so intertwined with ancient history offended his practical mind. Supernatural was one thing—legends and myths were another. And that, plus the growing impact of the fog—now visible to everyone—was feeding his rather vocal displeasure.

Derek, his mind somewhere else, responded automatically with a lecture. "Traditionally, Faeries have taken infants, not adults. Younger abductees are much more . . . adaptable. Those infants, or changelings, are replaced with children who usually sicken and die within months or, in an alternate version of the stories, with a carved doll or golem-like figure which mimics a human baby until the magic fades from it.

"But in cases of older humans, the stories are quite different. What we should keep in mind is that—if we can take David's recollections as truth—these do not seem to be fairies in the traditional Tinkerbelle sense, nor are they the singing-and-tale-telling elves so common in fantasy literature. They are Sidhe: the ancient warriors of Celtic legend. More often than not, the young human males entangled with the Court of Sidhe have not been abducted, per se. They are enticed, convinced to come of their own free will, according to a set of definite rules."

"Rules for abduction? What, only on every third Thursday?" Nick slumped deeper in his chair, clearly taking offense at what sounded like blame-the-victim mentality.

"Almost all mythology agrees that the fey of this

sort—elves, if you will—must follow certain traditions and rituals in their interactions with humans or else their bindings cannot work. And vice-versa, as shown by the legends of the swan maidens and selkies in which fey creatures may be captured by capturing their skins. All follow certain standard regulations, if you will. If those are not observed, then the being in question goes free."

"What, you're saying it was David's fault that they snatched him?" Nick snorted. "Come on, Derek. Does that kid look like he wanted to be wherever he was? I mean, running headlong through brambles and throwing yourself into the Pacific isn't exactly the sign of someone who's happy as a clam where he is."

"True. But we don't know—"

Alex jumped in, placing a spread of papers out on the table in front of her. "The problem is, with David not remembering any details of his life before he was taken, we're running short on facts. So anything we put together is just conjecture at this point, right?"

Derek nodded, and after a moment Nick jerked his head once in reluctant agreement.

"Okay then. As per Derek's instructions, I had the computer run a comprehensive search through the Legacy's database, including all the national missing persons reports for the past twenty years for anyone matching David's physical description. I focused on the East Coast, based on his accent, but spread the parameters up into eastern Canada, just to be on the safe side."

"And?"

Alex frowned at the hardcopy in front of her, her graceful hands spread out on top of the papers almost defensively.

"And?" Derek prodded. Her body language, obvious to one who knew her as well as her long-time mentor, screamed discomfort with what she had to say.

"And fortunately, the results came through before the phone lines went down. We came up with one possible match. David Carson, age twenty-three. College grad, Rutgers University, degree in political science. Unemployed, no current address at the time of disappearance. Last seen in New York City seven years ago."

"Seven years. Interesting number. Isn't the supernatural term of service supposed to be seven years?" Nick said, leaning back in his chair carefully, wincing a little as he hit a lingering bruise.

"That's Biblical, I think," Rachel said from her seat down the length of the table, in the process of pulling her blond hair back into a bun and securing it with one of the pencils she had been playing with earlier.

"But a number rife with supernatural and mythical implications nonetheless," Derek agreed, not missing the undercurrent of tension in the younger man's grousing.

Had he made a mistake, using Nick in this fashion? Putting the two of them together seemed to have reaped a definite, if dubious, harvest. Nick had taken to their young charge with an enthusiasm that was both like and curiously unlike him. Like, in that he was ever the champion of those in need, for his tough, bad-boy exterior barely hid the soul of a gentle soul. Unlike, for he had learned the hard way not to trust surface appearances. No matter how innocent they appeared—and perhaps especially not then.

"Seven is well-documented as a magical number, both pro and con," he continued, wondering how Nick was going to reconcile those two opposing instincts. And what damage it would leave if he couldn't.

"That's not the weird part," Alex said, flexing her slender fingers and forcing them to relax.

"More weirdness. What I live for," Nick said.

A grunt on the heels of that snideism indicated that Alex had kicked Nick under the table. He jumped slightly, leaning forward to rub at his shin. Ignoring his glare, she continued. "The weird part is that according to those records, David Carson was twenty-three when he disappeared."

"But that was seven years ago, you said. He barely looks that old now," Rachel protested, leaning forward as though to see what was written on the papers Alex was referring to.

"That is also covered in all the legends of mortals who go to live in the fey, or fairylands," Derek said. "Often they recall staying only one day and one night, and yet return home to discover an entire generation has grown and died in the length of that day. The story of Rip van Winkle is perhaps the most famous of American stories in that vein. And there are many legends of mortals taken as a faery's lover, who is warned to never touch foot on mortal soil again, lest they age and die in an instant."

"Well, he hasn't aged any since he's been here," Alex said. "So we can scrap that theory, right?"

Rachel frowned, remembering how frail David had been on the stairs that morning. But he had recovered almost immediately once they put some food into him. And, despite the emotional strain he had been under, he did not appear to her trained eye to be any older than when he had arrived.

Nick, bruised leg soothed, slumped back in his chair and picked up one of the sheets of hardcopy, folding it into a paper airplane, then flying it down the table before Alex could react. A full day of being caged in the house, staying on a knife's edge of tension without any hope of a break, was taking its toll on everyone, even the normally unflappable Derek, but most especially the kinetic ex-SEAL who normally required a good hard run around the island every morning before he could focus on the day's tasks. But this seemed a bit extreme, and

Derek filed that thought away for contemplation later, when he would have time for non-crisis discussions.

"Nick, please." Rachel was using her best mom-voice, knowing that it worked on the young man better than it ever did on her daughter Katherine.

"Sorry," he said with a shrug, leaning down the tabletop to retrieve the airplane and hand it back to Alex. "I wonder what could cause that kind of time distortion. I mean, are we talking another physical dimension here, some kind of magical fluctuation, a time warp, or what?"

"Let's do the Time Warp *agaaaaaiiin*," Alex singsonged softly, diverted by the idea.

The brief descent into silliness served its purpose, the aggravation level subsiding noticeably to everyone's relief. They were a well-trained team, and knowing how to blend humor into the most serious of situations had allowed them to tweak moods as needed, to smooth over rough patches like this; patches that might have derailed others.

"People have been searching for fairyland for as long as they've been telling stories about it," Rachel said, hauling the conversation back to the topic under discussion. "Avalon, Atlantis, Tir an Nog, the Land Under the Waves, just to name a few of the better known versions. So far, nobody has ever proven that such a place even exists."

"I think this has gone way beyond any academic research or discussion," Nick said. "I really don't care so much where they came from, as how we're going to get them to go back to wherever it is. And without David."

"But those appeared to be of this world, not another plane or dimension. They may be related, or they may be another type of fey completely," Derek said, thinking out loud.

"At a guess, from what David was able to tell us, and what's going on out there," and Rachel waved her arm to indicate beyond the walls of the House, "I have to agree with Derek. We're dealing with a different type of entity this time."

"What, so there are breeds of them? Do they hold a yearly Faerie Show at Westminster or Madison Square Garden?"

Alex nodded, agreeing with Rachel and completely ignoring Nick's comments. "The psychic residue I'm picking up was familiar enough to trigger something, probably what woke me up this morning, but it's not the same. If I were to put a name to these creatures, it wouldn't be faeries. I'd say they were closer to, well, elves, like Derek said. And not the cookie-making kind, either. Or Tolkien's, for that matter."

"David called them Sidhe," Derek added, "but there are a host of other creatures who would fit his descriptions just as well. My research suggests—"

Nick pushed his chair back and got up to pace the confines of the library, his hands jammed into the pockets of his jeans. His need to take action, caged by a lack of direction, was beginning to turn on itself. Tension sang from the set of his shoulders, the way his body canted forward as though about to charge a nonexistent fence.

The three others glanced at him, then looked away. Offering any kind of sympathy at this point would be useless—Nick would have to work through his frustration on his own and come back to the discussion when he was ready.

"Elves is as good a name for them as any," Derek continued smoothly. "For the moment. Or, if we feel like being traditional, we might refer to them as the Good Neighbors, although that hardly seems appropriate at this point."

Nick sniffed agreement from across the room.

"However we choose to categorize them, they are definitely of supernatural origin, and they have David convinced they are Sidhe, and that he has spent the past seven years of his life as a captive in their lands. However, we can't overlook the fact that neither his memory nor his judgment on this is completely trustworthy." Then Derek shrugged. "On the other hand, they are behaving true to type: aggressive, possessive, and vindictive."

"There's something else," Alex said. "According to these records, David wasn't in great shape physically when he disappeared. He was arrested a few times for vagrancy, didn't have a job or even a listed address. Odds are pretty good that he was living on the street. And there are records of him being treated at the King Street Clinic for general malnutrition and heroin addiction several times over the period of a year or so before he vanished."

"What? He's clean, I can assure you of that," Rachel said, her professional pride stirred. "I wouldn't have missed signs of that. Or malnutrition. And there's no way someone in that kind of shape could have swum here. I don't care how good a swimmer they were." Her words rang with certainty, but her eyes were shadowed by a hint of doubt. She had seen signs of it, in the way he held himself, the way he didn't seem to trust his own senses. But the drug screens had come back negative. So which did she trust, her science or her own gut knowledge?

"Now, yes," Derek agreed, taking the folded printout, opening it, and studying the information printed there intently. "But he has been in the hands of some sort of magical creatures for seven years, no matter how little mark those years may have left on him in terms of aging. We cannot discount their influence on his health." He put that sheet down and picked up another, then picked up the first sheet again and compared the two.

"If so, they've got one hell of a health care program," Nick opined, coming back to reclaim his chair, turning it around and straddling it, his elbows propped on the back. "I mean, you don't just wake up one morning and say, hey, I don't think I need drugs any more. That would have to be one serious detox program."

"Indeed," Derek said thoughtfully, placing both sheets back down on the table and rubbing absently at the post–five-o'clock stubble on his cheek. "Interesting. Sidhe or no, they seem to have kept him in better shape than he was before and are apparently loathe to lose him now."

"If you discount the beatings and scarring," Rachel reminded them, coming back into the conversation. "Those aren't seven years old, I can assure you of that!"

"Yes. The scars. Curious. I wish we had some way of getting the other side of the story."

"What, you mean theirs?" Rachel pointed a finger toward the window, now blanketed with a light gray fog that looked backlit, despite the fact that her watch indicated the sun would have set some time before.

"Yes. I am uncomfortable taking only one man's word on a situation. Especially a man who cannot remember very important details."

"I don't know, Derek," Nick said. "They didn't seem too eager to talk last time. Matter of fact, I'd say we got a big, bright, neon shut-up sign."

"Or perhaps, we were asking the wrong questions."

Had anyone looked at the screen displaying the feed from David's room, they would have seen that the room was empty, the bed covers tossed back, clothing scattered across the room with the casual negligence of someone who had never paid for their belongings. Of a child. Or a teenager in a particularly foul mood.

The sound of water falling nearby was cut off, and a thumping, swearing noise replaced it. Then a door opened into the bedroom, releasing mists of steam into the air. David left the bathroom, clad only in a towel wrapped loosely around his lean hips, another towel in his hands. The scars Alex and Derek had noted earlier were more prominent now, his skin flushed pink from the heat of his shower. The pale white marks criss-crossed his chest; short, blunt marks tearing his flesh, the scars testifying to how badly they had healed.

One particularly long scar swung from his right pectorals down across his belly and slid around his left hip before ending with a wicked flourish. It was too fine, too long to be a knife stroke, but only someone well versed in weaponry could have identified it as the mark of a bullwhip wielded with exquisite skill. And, unlike the others, it had been treated, and healed without puckering edges or lumps. David seemed completely oblivious to his disfigurement, moving unselfconsciously through the room with a strength that would have reassured Rachel, had she seen it.

He used the towel in his hands to dry his hair, rubbing at it vigorously, but never allowing the folds of white terry to obscure his face, or his line of sight. His movements were casual, relaxed, but there was a tension in his muscles that spoke of long-term wariness, like an herbivore currently at rest, but always alert for potential threats.

Nick would have recognized them. As both a soldier and the child of abuse.

Walking to the dresser, he dropped the towel onto the floor and stared in the mirror. His long brown hair, still damp, clung to the sides of his pale, full-cheeked face and made him look even younger. He scowled at his reflection. Dark brows pulled down over his chocolate-brown eyes, and his jaw firmed. But the result didn't seem to please him. Snorting once, he relaxed his features, which immediately reassumed the open, appealing countenance he had worn earlier when talking to Rachel and Derek. It was important that they trust him. Important that they care for him and want to protect him.

Moving away from the dresser, he stooped to reclaim the sweatpants from where he had tossed them on the floor. Disdaining underwear, he dropped the other towel from around his waist and slid the pants on. Tightening the drawstring so that they wouldn't fall off his hips, more slender than Nick's frame, he stopped abruptly, his head going up like a deer suddenly scenting a predator.

Ignoring the shirt crumpled by his foot, David glided across the room, cautious but unable to stop himself. The window seemed to call to him, beckoning to him, calling him like the Loreli, the most dangerous of all the Sirens. Confident in his own protections, the thin line of metal scraps lining the floor's edges, he went closer.

There were sounds in the mist. Impossible sounds coming through the thick stone defenses. Seeping through the metal wiring and magical protections. Inaudible sounds, nothing the human voice could produce. Nothing the human ear could discern.

His fingers touched the cool wooden frame of the window, and he shuddered, the tremor working its way up his arms and down his spine. The view outside the window was obscured, the fog heavy and soft, pressing up against the window like cotton batting. Even through the worst weather, it should have been possible to see the lights of San Francisco from there. He knew that somehow. But there was nothing. Only a pale, cool gray. And the sounds he couldn't hear.

David shuddered again. His fingers clenched on the windowsill, and it seemed for a moment as though he were fighting with himself. Then his eyes closed, his shoulders bowed, and his head moved forward until his forehead touched the window itself, resting his entire body weight on that slight contact. The position was one of exhaustion, of resignation, but the play of muscles along his back showed the tension within. A drop of sweat slid down the side of his neck despite his shower and the cool temperature of the room.

Outside, on the other side of the thick glass, the fog shifted, pressing in as though in response to his appearance. There was a flicker, a darkening of the elements, and then a shimmer of lights appeared within the fog, flickering blue and green and red and gold. They hung back a moment, then their brightness intensified, and they swam forward, coming straight up to the glass. One, brighter than the others, flared a painfully intense blue.

David's eyes opened as though he had been jabbed with something sharp, and he looked up right into the blue light.

"Mary, Mother of God," he swore, jumping back from the window, and looking around wildly for a weapon of some sort.

The lights flared again, filling the room with an unearthly glow. The mist swirled, creating the illusion of a face; long, high-cheek boned, with dark hollows where the eyes should have been. The skin was stretched like parchment, almost translucent. Living, but unearthly; inhuman. A malevolent leer stretched the narrow lips, showing small, white, even teeth.

David took another step back, almost tripping over the towel on the floor. "No! No, you are not allowed in here. This is a refuge, and you cannot pass. I know that. I know that and you can't trick me into letting you in."

But his voice was shaky, his bravado that of a little boy who has outrun the town bullies to the safety of his front porch, but isn't entirely sure that porch is so safe.

The face said nothing, the glow fading, the sounds disappearing, until all that could be heard was the rasping of his breath. Downstairs, he knew, there was safety, protection. But he was unable to yell, unable to call for aid.

Instead, he stared into the face, through the dubious protection of the glass, and the face stared into him.

One, two, three, four minutes passed, and David's nerve snapped. He lunged forward, yanking on the cord that brought the shades down with a snap and a clatter. Trembling, he retreated to the chair by the door, and sat there, staring at the blocked window, waiting.

Some time later, he roused from his uneasy doze at a sound in the hallway outside. But it was only the light tread of feet, coming up the stairs and stopping by his door.

"David?"

Rachel. The sudden flush of relief he felt was completely out of proportion.

"Yes?" he said softly, not rising from his chair.

"I just wanted to make sure you . . . that you didn't need anything."

That I was okay, he translated mentally. *That I hadn't upped and disappeared while they weren't looking. Not likely. Not with Them outside, just waiting for me to make a mistake. No, I think I'll stay right here.*

"No, thank you. I'm fine. Are you all turning in for the night?"

On the other side of the door, Rachel let out a soft laugh. "Well, I am. When the brain stops coming up with anything coherent, I've generally taken that as a sign to get some sleep. And Derek turned in a while back, although I don't doubt he's still up reading. And Nick and Alex are still working downstairs, if you decide that you want some company."

"Probably not." The thought of Nick's easy, undemanding companionship was appealing, but he was less sure about Alex. She looked at him oddly, and that made him uneasy. "Sleep sounds like a good idea. Good night, Rachel. And . . . thank you."

"You're welcome, David. Sleep well."

Katherine Corrigan was neither stupid, nor particularly dense. In fact, she knew that she was smarter than the average bear, to use Nick's phrase. And she had long ago figured out that her mom's work involved a lot more than poking around in peoples' heads to see why they did bad things or were unhappy all the time. So when she had to go away on business, on Luna Foundation business, Kat worried.

Not a lot, really, because mom said she was going to the house on Angel Island, and Nick and Alex and Derek would be there and the four of them could handle lots of weird stuff. But just enough that she wanted to talk to her mom before she went to bed. Just to . . . make sure.

Only the phone number for the house wasn't working, and neither was the secured line Nick had told her about, that went into the main office and she wasn't supposed to use except in really serious emergencies.

Well, okay. Phone lines could go down. Just because they hadn't had a storm or any kind of power outage didn't mean things couldn't go wrong.

"But that doesn't explain why her cell phone isn't picking up," she said to herself, reaching for another brownie off the platter on the table in front of her.

"Picking up what?" Mrs. Frants asked, coming into the kitchen. "And no more of those before bed, young lady. That much sugar and you'll never get to sleep."

"My mom's phone," Kat said, dropping the brownie with a longing look. "It keeps saying that she's out of range. But that's silly. She's just over on the island, right? That's within range."

"Maybe there's something in the air that's messing with the signals. You know, weird weather, government tests, aliens coming down to abduct people . . ."

Kat giggled. Mrs. Frants could be really silly, for an adult. That's why it wasn't so bad being baby-sat. Besides, Mrs. F never once asked her if she had finished her homework or anything. She just assumed that Kat had done all her work before goofing off.

Which she had. The stuff they gave her to do in school was easy. It was a lot more fun to hang out with Nick or Alex at the Foundation, and work with them on grown-up stuff. Like the computers. Hmmm. Maybe she could get through to Alex's e-mail. Only if she didn't pick up, Kat wouldn't know, and even if Alex did pick up and sent e-mail back, Kat wouldn't be able to pick it up until morning, and by then her mom would be home and . . .

"I'm sure that it's nothing, dear." Mrs. F was saying now. "When your mother called me, she said that she might be very busy tonight. Perhaps she forgot to turn the phone on."

"Maybe." Mom did that sometimes, spaced out totally on anything that wasn't the immediate problem. Especially if she knew that her daughter was home, safe, with someone to look after her.

But Kat wasn't convinced. Not entirely. Something had been tingling at the back of her head all night, like static. Derek had told her to listen for stuff like that. It might be nothing, he had said. Or it might be really important.

Covering the brownies with tin foil and putting them away on the counter, Kat turned almost automatically in the direction of Angel Island. Closing her eyes and focusing on the mental image of the huge old house, she sent out a wish.

"Be careful, Mom. All of you, be careful. I want you all to come home safe."

SEVEN

The waters around Angel Island churned slightly, as though stirred by the wind, although the rest of the surf was calm in the cool evening air. Whitecaps formed briefly, then faded back into green-blue water. If someone were to connect the whitecaps, it would form a staggering line, leading up to the rocky shore, as though something were moving through the depths, up onto dry land.

The mist tightened in places, forming inpenetrable oblongs of condensation, practically invisble in the fallen darkness. Dim lights flickered within each oblong, and a faint humming noise started, as though many voices far away were murmuring to each other.

On the ground, a squirrel stopped, startled, then turned tail and fled. A crab, less discerning, scuttled along the sandy soil until it reached the nearest oblong. It stopped, as though it had run into a stone wall, and started forward again. The oblong twitched, more the whisper of a movement than an actual physical action, and the crab scuttled back several feet before deciding that discretion was the better part of crustacean valor and disappearing down a quickly-dug hole.

There were twelve oblongs now, several feet wide and almost ten feet high, each giving the impression of rapid movement while staying completely still. Someone prone to motion sickness would have found the experience of looking at them to be profoundly nauseating. One moved forward in a soundless, sinewy glide, then stopped, pulled up hard almost exactly the same way the crab had been. It was as though a warning sign had appeared: *this far, and no further*.

The humming noise grew louder, individual voices almost discernable. Angry, and cajoling, bitter and cool, sibilants and harsh consonants, tangles in a speech that was in no way human . . .

It had been a very long day, and an even longer night. Slowly, the residents let the tension and uncertainty of the past twelve hours wear them down, overcoming the between-the-shoulder-blades twitchiness which had kept them going well into the night. Humans simply weren't designed to operate at peak momentum like that for more than a brief period of danger. Afterwards, they needed to recharge. To escape, if only through a few hours of sleep.

If anything wanted to come in, the alarms would wake them . . . although what they could do then, nobody could suggest.

Beginning with the library, the work lights flickered out one by one, until at three A.M., the great stone house was dark and silent, only the hum of power lines and psychic energy indicating any kind of sentry still standing guard.

Even Derek had finally given in to the needs of his

body. Carefully putting aside his books and research notes, he crawled into bed and turned out the light on the nightstand. But even exhausted, his mind couldn't give up working, and his sleep was not a calm one.

Eventually, however, his movements stilled, and for an instant an observer might have thought him peacefully resting. But then his broad forehead creased, and his shoulders tensed, flinching as though to avoid a blow. It passed, and his chest rose and fell in a normal rhythm. Then:

"No. No, I won't."

His whispered plea echoed throughout the bedroom, filling the empty space for a brief instance before it was swallowed by the silence. His head turned on the pillow, negating whatever was being whispered to his subconscious.

"No. No, I won't!"

Derek sat upright in bed, his pajamas soaked with sweat, his graying hair disordered and matted in places from classic pillow-head.

"I won't . . . what?" he said, his voice scratchy and sleep-fogged. But already, whatever had been disturbing him had faded away, and nothing he tried could call the memories back.

He reached out and turned on the light, blinking at the sudden illumination. But the glow from the lamp revealed nothing other than the normal furnishings of his bedroom: desk and bookcase, wardrobe, leather armchair holding the black-and-red stuffed bear Alex had inflicted upon him last birthday. The clock blinked at him, the digits flashing forward another minute: 3:54.

"A nightmare." His voice was stronger now, but it didn't sound convinced, or convincing, even to himself, and he could practically hear the snickers of whatever it was that lurked outside. Self-denial had never been one of his stronger skills. Even assuming it was a reaction to the stress of the previous day, a dream of that magnitude, to one with his sensitivities, was often an indicator of something more.

Derek shook his head, running fingers through his hair in an attempt to tame it. Perhaps he should see if Alex was experiencing the same indicators . . .

He looked at the clock on the nightstand once more, and shook his head again, more roughly, forcing himself to lie back down. No. Best to let her get what sleep she could. Even if this were some kind of warning, it was highly unlikely that they could—

The floor underneath him rumbled, the supposedly earthquake-proof foundations of the Legacy House shaken by some tremendous force, like a snow globe in the hand of a toddler.

"Dear God." Derek sat back up again, shoving the covers down and reaching for the clothes he had discarded barely an hour before.

So much for good intentions.

Rachel had crawled into bed, intending on studying up on the few materials she had on-hand that dealt with amnesia. Texts on that subject, interspersed with several dog-eared pamphlets on drug use, addiction, and rehabilitation techniques, were scattered across the coverlet, an open spiral notebook covered with her neatly-written commentary.

Propped up on pillows stuffed behind her back, reading glasses perched low on her nose, her mouth was hanging open slightly and a gentle snore now rose from her throat. It was a testament to Rachel's unshakable Southern upbringing that even in sleep she had a distinctly ladylike take on what should have been a comical pose.

The first rumble barely made it through to her sleep-cottoned awareness. But when the heavy wooden-frame bed slid almost a foot across the floor, she bolted upright, falling out of bed before her eyes were completely open. The books fell with a heavy thud on the floor, the open notebook getting tangled in and half-covered by the blanket. Her pen had leaked onto the white sheets, leaving a deep black stain. She noticed none of this.

"Kat?"

Even now, after all that had occurred since joining the Legacy, her immediate reaction to awakening in the night was that something had happened to her daughter. Katherine would be in college, grown and living on her own, before that ever changed. If, in fact, it ever did. Some instincts die hard.

But once her feet hit the floor, Rachel awoke completely, recalling where she was, and under what conditions she had fallen asleep. Clad in an old, worn, button-down shirt that had belonged to her husband, she frowned at the floor as though trying to recall what it was that had woken her.

"Not an earthquake, certainly . . ."

A quick turn and two steps brought her to the nearest window, where she had pulled the curtains shut against the sight of that living, threatening mist when she undressed a few hours before.

"Come on, Rachel, do it," she urged herself, irritated with her own hesitation. "It can't reach you through the glass, for heaven's sake." At least, they didn't think it could—no, if that were possible, it would have gotten in already. The wards were doing their job. It should be perfectly safe to look outside . . .

Swallowing hard once, she reached out and pulled the curtain aside, as though expecting—despite her brave words—something to jump out through the glass pane.

Heavy gray fog swirled against the glass, pushing and fading in slow turns, almost like a normal fog-bound San

Francisco morning on Angel Island. It had thickened in the hours since she last looked, the physical presence now matching the psychic one Alex had tried describing to her. The only thing missing was the low honk of foghorns connecting them however tenuously to the outside world.

"But, if what Derek theorized was true," she said, looking but not really seeing the scene any more, "the outside world didn't know that the foghorns were supposed to be blaring."

Kat had no idea what was keeping her mother from coming home.

"Oh, my poor baby . . ."

The room rumbled again, floorboards vibrating, and Rachel snapped out of her reverie. Whatever was going on, earthquake or not, it was unlikely to be unrelated to their current situation. Coincidence only went so far, even on Angel Island. Which meant there would be yet another emergency session forming downstairs.

A knock on the door, and then it opened before she could tell whoever it was to come in. A white ceramic mug held in a hand attached to a slender bare arm came around the door. Steam rose off the top of the mug.

"One coffee, too hot to drink just yet. Careful the next tremor doesn't make you spill anything."

Rachel went to the door, taking the offering gratefully from Alex, who was already dressed in jeans and a sleeveless knit top, looking far too awake and alert. "You're a godsend, did you know that?" She savored the scent of the French Roast, turning away in order to get dressed, then stopped. "Next tremor? How many have there been?"

But Alex had already left, presumably on her next mission of mercy.

"Huh." Rachel sipped her coffee, reaching with one hand for the top drawer of the heavily carved dresser which held her sweaters. "I guess I do sleep as heavily as Kat claims."

Fairies. Abductees. Rituals and curses and supernatural contracts. And in the middle of it all, one scared young man with the scars of abuse marked inside and out. What did it all mean? Where was the thread that would pull it all into shape, make the answers easy to find?

Nick had long ago trained himself to ignore unanswered questions long enough to be able to catch much-needed sleep. So, despite the chaos still whirling in his brain, he had crawled into bed around midnight with the plan of sleeping until his usual five A.M. wake up. When he opened his eyes again, hopefully his brain would have sorted out the nonessential crap and left him with a clear set of objectives. Or at least slightly better organized chaos.

Jolting awake into a bad imitation of a 70s disaster movie an hour earlier than planned, though, didn't do much for his thoughts. Or, for that matter, his mood. Damn elves. Elfie-welfie sword-wearing pointy-eared cookie-baking . . .

He lay there, completely awake and alert, and let off several of his more treasured swear words until the room stopped shaking around him.

"Thank you." He wasn't quite sure who he was thanking, but that didn't change any of the gratitude in his tone.

Getting out of bed, he walked carefully to avoid cutting the soles of his bare feet on the shards of red glass that littered the floor. They were the remnants of a water jar Rachel had found on one of her antiquing jaunts, a halfway decent piece of Depression-era glassware.

"I really liked that pitcher," he muttered, thankful that it hadn't actually had any water in it, since he had drunk the last glassful before going to bed.

Reaching a relatively safe spot on the floor, Nick opened the low cedar chest against the wall and pulled out a pair of jeans, which he slipped on over the briefs he had worn to bed. Refusing to walk back across the minefield of the floor to get socks, he shoved his feet into a pair of docksiders and grabbed a sweatshirt off the week-old pile of clean laundry still waiting to be put away.

"Later," he promised the remainder, hoping that there would be a later to deal with things like laundry. Putting it out of his mind, he headed for the door, reaching out to grab the knob.

"Careful!" but Alex's warning came half a second too late, followed by a startled, high-pitched yelp and another swearword from him, quickly bitten off. They both looked at the coffee splattered over his formerly-clean sweatshirt and jeans, and sighed.

"There's more downstairs. Coffee, I mean. No time to change, Derek wants us all—"

"Downstairs as soon as possible. I figured that out myself. About the shake-n-bake attempt, with us as the chicken, I assume. Any clues?"

"You get one guess."

"Our foggy friends?"

"Bingo. Get moving."

David was already awake. He had managed a series of cat naps throughout the night, dozing uneasily for a few minutes only to open his eyes and stare suspiciously at the window. Not being able to see what was out there didn't make it any less vivid. He knew. Even through the thick walls and the drawn shades, he knew.

They were here. On the island.

No matter what form they took, he would always feel them. Like a chill on the skin. Like mercury in his bloodstream.

Like the poison he had craved. The poison they had so easily replaced with yet another endless, disgusting craving.

No, the heavy shroud of fog made no difference. If you listened carefully, and knew what to pay attention to, you could hear them, slithering around the walls, searching out weaknesses, wheedling for an invitation. But he was a good learner, if not a very fast one, and now he was wise to them. Wise to what they could do to him—and what they could not. So long as he stayed here, in this room, under protection of so much warding, he was safe.

And there was safety here, even beyond what he had done to protect himself. He could feel it, after so much time with Them. He had seen it as a beacon of safety far in the distance, felt the human warmth of it. The entire house was heavy with wardings; some effective, some not, like a subtle flicker of lightning in the distance, or the purr of an engine underfoot.

For a moment, he toyed with the idea of confiding in Nick, at least. His earlier fears cracked slightly under the unaccustomed weight of other warm bodies around him, made him wonder if there wasn't another way. But even as the thought entered his head, hard-won paranoia slammed down on it, crushing it. So they were mortal. So they said they would protect him with their lives. So what? It would be a useless gesture, for no mortal could stand against Them, physically.

No, there was only one way Nick and the others could help him. And honesty was not the way to invoke it. Not when so much depended on their sincerity . . .

There was also the risk that someone else here might invite Them in, foolishly allow them access all unknowing, but he didn't think that would happen. While he might not trust mortals either, no place would be so carefully constructed, so well-warded, if the people living within didn't know how to protect themselves from the beings hunched outside.

And if some of the protections in the stones felt like they were intended to keep things *in*, rather than out, well, so long as they didn't affect him, he wouldn't worry about whatever it was they were guarding. Live and let live, that was his motto now.

David nodded, wrapping his arms more securely around his drawn-up knees and leaning against the bed's headboard. It didn't matter. He was safe here, in this house that glowed with the warmth of the sun even after nightfall. Safe within the line of metal that crackled just outside the range of his hearing, defiant with the cold precision of science.

Yes. Everything would work the way it had to. Derek, the older man with those old-looking eyes, he *knew*. He knew what They were. And Nick, he wouldn't let anyone harm him. He had promised, given his word. Even Rachel and Alex, they would take his side, mortal to mortal. They had to, they couldn't be as cruel as her.

He hoped that his newfound protectors were strong enough to do what had to be done. He was betting his life, his soul, his very freedom on it. That he could stay here until it was safe. Until he was safe. Until They gave up and left him alone.

The wind tapped on his window again, as it had been all night, and David felt a shiver touch along his spine. Who was he trying to kid? They wouldn't just give up and go away. Not ever. He could do nothing but cower here, like a rabbit under brush waiting for the dogs to go by. Only in his case, the dogs had caught his scent and were circling around, waiting for the moment to pounce, with only the threat of thorns keeping them at bay. They would keep sniffing, keep trying, until somewhere a defense fell, and the thorns were proved useless. And then they would be upon him. He would never be safe again.

When the mirror on the wall began to shake under the first of the attacks, David instinctively rolled out of the bed, looking for a place to hide, to escape.

But there was no place else left to run to.

EIGHT

*There's something that I'm not remembering. Some-
thing that's important, so important it dances outside
my conscious grasp, taunting me with my inability to
recall it. A solution, or a cause and effect . . . some rev-
elation which will bring me back to the proper path . . .*

Derek put down his pen and closed his journal, staring
at the walls of the library, as though looking for solace
within the physical weight of their bindings and paper.

The great stone mansion which housed the San Francisco chapter of the Legacy had seen many different
manifestations in its time, from demons to evil encased
in human flesh, from ghosts to cursed Scotsmen rein-
carnated as dark-dwelling sprites with swords. All dangerous, all out to destroy them. But in all that time, it
had never felt this sort of assault on its well-set stones.
Neither entirely physical, nor psychic, but somewhere in
between, the members of the Legacy could find no way
to hold it off, much less stop it. And it was all the more

dangerous for the fact that it seemed completely oblivious to them, intent only on the one apparently helpless human sheltered within those walls.

Turning in his chair, Derek looked up at the monitor which showed David pacing restlessly in his room.

Who was this young man, that he should be the focus of all this? What secrets was he hiding beneath that bland, walled-off exterior? Frowning, Derek twisted the heavy signet ring on his finger in a gesture that seemed automatic, a worry-stone of sorts. If that ring was the physical sign of his position as leader of this chapter of the Legacy, then the weight which sometimes seemed to settle on his shoulders was the less tangible but no less real reminder. He had been the one to allow David refuge within these walls, so it was his responsibility to ferret out the truth and bring this to a conclusion. As of yet, the threads he had spun were still incomplete, the results uncertain. He couldn't shake the feeling that David was holding something back, some piece of information that, once shared, would give him the solution he needed.

Or maybe you're just looking for excuses? He's still terrified. That much is obvious. Stop assigning anything more sinister to his natural caution.

Another shiver passed through the building, and there was a crash from the upper level of the library. Derek winced in silent regret, his train of thought derailed. Effort had been made to protect the more valuable and powerful of the fragile objects d'art, but not everything could be adequately secured. There simply wasn't the time or manpower available.

The last tremor subsided, and his gaze passed over his companions, gauging them almost unconsciously. He didn't doubt their strength or their determination, but as proctor of this House, it was also his responsibility to ever monitor their commitment, their dedication to battling the forces which opposed them.

Monitor, and enhance it, as much as possible. But for the moment at least, it looked as though they were doing as well as could be hoped for. In the half hour or so since they had all gathered in the library, the initial reactions of fear and uncertainty had faded into a battleweary resignation tempered with anger. Resignation, because they could not do anything other than wait and watch. Anger because . . . well, because they could do nothing other than wait and watch.

"Hey," Rachel said, swatting at Alex, who was reaching across the table to cut a chunk of cheese off the platter someone had scrounged from the kitchen. "Watch the crumbs."

Legacy members were trained to take action against evil. Not to sit trapped in their own home and twiddle their thumbs. And his team in particular had made a name for themselves as . . . Well, impetuous. Or, if you listened to William Sloan, "short-tempered, bull-headed and terminally stubborn."

Alex made a face at Rachel, but thankfully didn't make a comment in return. Stuffing the cheese and cracker into her mouth, she returned to her place across the room, and the quiet hum of concentration fell over the room again.

At the time of the comment, Derek had pointed out to Sloan that these were descriptions which could have sketched Sloan himself to a tee, and gotten a gruff "harumph" in return. But not before the other man had allowed a smile to lighten his glowering features a hint. It was comforting, in a way, to know that whatever happened to them here, Sloan would not rest until he had tracked down the source and—

"Stop that thought there," he muttered to himself. No one had died yet, and Derek intended to make sure that it stayed that way. And even if that worst-case scenario were to occur, what could Sloan, or any of the Legacy, for that matter, do? If the force outside managed to break through and take back with it what it was here for, it would be over. No matter that David had somehow managed to cross that boundary between worlds—there was no guarantee that anyone here could. There would be no way to extract justice for their deaths across that hidden border, even assuming their assailants left any trail for the Legacy to follow. For all his journal entries, for all the notes he was certain Rachel was taking, there was nothing they knew which would allow them to access whatever border David had escaped over. Not once the young man had been retaken.

He shook off those negative thoughts and turned his attention back to the matters he could influence. Sitting back in his chair, he steepled his fingers in front of him and looked around the room.

Rachel was still immersed in her third cup of coffee, alternating between inhaling the steam and sipping the liquid as she sorted once again through the sheaf of notes she had put together, both her own research and his own, on the legend, myths, and descriptions of fey folk which might be of use. Occasionally, she got up and browsed the shelves, not looking so much as reassuring herself that she wasn't merely running in place.

Alex, also nose-down in her caffeine, took a sip, then held it away from the keyboard, maneuvering the touch-pad with her free hand to highlight a section of the house schematics she was discussing over the intercom with Nick in the Control Room. The surface of Alex's coffee quivered in the aftershocks, but didn't spill over the edges.

"Careful," Derek warned, and she nodded without really hearing him.

Normally, liquids were not allowed near the electronics, not to mention several of the books they had pulled out from the library's extensive shelves, but he doubted any of them would be able to function without the thick sludge Rachel specialized in to settle their nerves. Derek made a mental note that he should start tracking their consumption of caffeine, then considered the possible repercussions if he told them to cut back and discarded the idea.

"Nick's right, Derek," Alex said, looking over her shoulder at him. "There's no way anything should be doing this." She paused as another shiver rumbled through the house, tossing an entire shelf of books onto the floor. Everyone winced that time, but nobody rose to replace them. After the first few disturbances, it became apparent that any attempt at cleaning up would be a waste of energy until this was over. Thankfully, this time there were no disasters of the breakable kind. That Derek could hear, anyway.

As Nick and Alex discussed the ways to combat an attack that was, in Nick's words, neither fish nor foul nor good red meat, Derek once again gave thanks to the secured rooms in the basement. With luck, the esoteric items contained therein would be safe no matter what punishment their unfriendly visitor handed out.

Which made him wonder, once again, about this attack. The hows, if not the whys. And leaving aside the everpresent questions about the who or whats.

How did they manage to get through the wardings?

While the others searched for a way to stop it, his scholar's mind, the part not watching the display screens or contemplating his coworkers, wrestled with the question. The power which was shaking the well-situated stones under their feet wasn't geological, because the sensors in the ground beyond the foundations showed no disruption. Just as the weather buoys reported no fog, he reminded himself, flinching slightly as his own coffee sloshed over the rim of his mug and burned his hand.

They rode the tremor out, even Rachel lifting her head from her notes this time to watch the computer screen as it displayed electronically the structural health of the building.

"Are we still here?" Rachel asked, only half-joking.

"Still here," Nick said, coming out through the reactivated holographic doorway. "None of the quakes, for lack of a better word, have been enough to do any severe damage. But you peck at even the best shell long enough, the snail gets eaten."

"Oh, nice image," Alex said, grimacing.

"He's right, though. That's what they're doing."

David stood in the library's entrance, unsteady but grim-faced. Derek had the fleeting thought that the boy—man—finally looked his actual age. Lines marred the prettiness of his round face, and exhaustion had hollowed his cheeks slightly.

Rachel stood, advancing on her patient like a general heading to battle. "David, you shouldn't be out of bed again so soon. This isn't the best place for you to be—"

David smiled wryly, brushing her off. "Like there's anyplace safe right now?"

"He has a point," Nick said. "Better to see what's coming than hide under the bed."

"Sez you," Alex retorted.

David interrupted before they could start another round of friendly squabbling. "Look. I . . . whatever is happening out there, it's because of me. They want me. So sitting upstairs alone just isn't my idea of being safe or having fun. It may not be any safer down here, but if They . . . if They break through, I don't want to be alone. Okay?"

He looked at Rachel, then at Derek, having clearly figured out who the decision makers were in the group.

His tone was hopeful-plaintive, like a dog might use if it wanted the scraps off your plate but didn't think you liked him enough to feed him. It was a child's voice, the please-be-my-friend wheedle you used the first day on the playgound.

Derek rubbed the back of his neck with his free hand, suddenly unbearably weary, irritated with his own judgments. The coffee wasn't helping. It was a good sign that David was trying to integrate himself with the group, take action against what was threatening him—wasn't it?

A quick look at Rachel gave him no aid, her face quietly composed and completely neutral. And he already knew where Nick and Alex stood, respectively. This one was up to him. As, in the end, so many decisions were.

"I suspect, against my better judgment, that David is correct. While there may not be safety in numbers, there is no reason he should not be included in our discoveries. They do, after all, impact on him greatly."

Besides which, the more David felt like a member of the group, the more he would have invested in their continued survival, and the more likely he would be to fill in missing details. Ideally.

"We'll impact him one way or the other," Alex muttered, fiddling with the controls of one of the monitors. Nick frowned at her, clearly offended by her semi-sarcastic tone when it came to their guest.

"Look, why don't you sit down before you fall over?" he said, leaving her side and taking David by the elbow. "Here. Comfiest chair in the entire house, tested and proven by just about everyone."

Rachel watched the two young men, a frown now creasing her brow. But when Derek raised an eyebrow of his own, to ask what the matter was, she shook her head, indicating that it was nothing. He accepted her reservations as he had his own, without comment. But they both stood there, watching as Nick handled David like an invalid, settling him in the new chair and handing him a pile of books to go through, to make him feel like part of the team.

Those volumes were unlikely to be of use, hence the fact that nobody had done more than scan them and set them aside, but it was a good, considered gesture; one Derek normally would not have expected of the former SEAL, who tended to be more brusque in his dealings with people outside the Legacy.

But then, he had thrown them together precisely for this reaction, to make use of Nick's own troubled childhood, to create a bond between the two men that they might be able to use in ferreting out a solution locked somewhere in David's mind and memory. He had done it deliberately, with misgivings aforethought, and having weighed the probable good enough to offset the possible damages.

So why, now that it was working beyond his expectations, was he suddenly so concerned?

"Because maybe it's working too well?" Alex said, leaving her computers to come stand by his elbow.

"Reading my mind again?" he asked, half-joking.

She didn't smile. "No need to. I know you, and I know Nick. And I knew that you wouldn't be deliberately pushing all of Nick's buttons like this if you didn't think it would help. Because if David has been lying to us—"

"Then Nick will be torn between helping his new friend and finding out the truth."

"I only hope that's all he's torn between."

"Yes." He looked at her, hoping for some reassurances, but she merely shook her head and went back to watching the monitors.

And Derek, deeply unsettled, walked away from the

scene of the young man thumbing with careful concentration through a heavy book. Standing by the one uncovered window, the Proctor watched the tiny colored flickers within the fog as it swirled and danced just out of reach. It was enticing, almost hypnotic, and for an instant he could almost hear the voices from his dream; sweet, sorrowful voices calling him to open the window and reach out to them . . .

"Derek! We've got a breakthrough in the defenses!"

Nick's shout broke through the vague catatonia Derek had slipped into, and he came back to himself with a start, just before his hand made contact with the windowpane.

The younger man's shout had brought everyone to their feet, moving to gather around Alex's small screen, which still displayed a schemata of the house. A stern glance from Derek made David stay where he was, pouting. But Derek had no time to waste on explaining his reasons for keeping the young man away—even to himself. A section of the schemata, normally outlined in cool blue, was now showing a sharp red-brown.

"That's the sub-basement," Rachel said, shooting a worried glance at Derek. "Where . . ." She trailed off, obviously not wanting to say more where David could hear. They could have moved this back into the Control Room, giving them more security, as well as access to better resolution terminals, but . . .

But the whole point was to make David feel less isolated, not more.

"If they break open into that room," Nick said, his hands poised uselessly over the keyboard, "if they let anything loose . . ."

Alex, who had been jiggling with the bank of monitors on the other side of the library that were normally used for database searches within the House itself, came over to stand just behind Nick, watching over his shoulder. Her face showed that she was torn between wanting to push Nick out of his chair and do something, and knowing that she would be just as useless if she were the one sitting there.

Instead, she moved toward the main desk, as though to pick up the in-house phone. But she checked her movement mid-stride, realizing at that moment that there was no one for her to call. She flexed her fingers, aching for something to grab onto, something to do. But there was nothing. Even assuming the impossible, that they could arrive at the storage area in time, what could they do? How could any of them stand against a force that was showing it could indeed crack them open like a clam?

But even as that thought registered in everyone's brain—that they had in a very real way been breached— the red lines faded to a muddier, more muted brown.

"They're backing off," Nick breathed in shock. "They're avoiding the storage rooms." He looked up at Alex, then at Derek, who was still staring at the screen. The proctor's face was once again a composed blank, but they had all worked together too long not to sense the mind working furiously underneath that exterior.

"Derek, what's going on? Not that I'm complaining, mind you, but what's up with that?"

"They know what's in there," Rachel said quietly. "They sensed it somehow, and they chose to avoid it. They backed off because otherwise . . . They didn't want to let those magics loose any more than we do."

"That's crazy," Nick protested, even as the proof was displayed on the screen in front of him. "Why should they care about what damage those things might do?"

"I think," Derek said slowly, finally, "that we may have been overlooking some important details."

"Like what?"

But Derek only shook his head, watching the brown

lines fade back to the cool blue that indicated a security he no longer felt.

"Like the fact that anything that could do that," and Alex indicated the screen, "could have probably done a lot worse, a lot faster."

"No one's been hurt," Rachel said suddenly. "The house, yes, there's been damage, but nobody's been injured by any of it. Even when that statue fell over—"

"It barely missed me!" Nick protested.

"By a good meter," Derek corrected him. "And you're right, Rachel. No one has gotten more than a bruise, and that was only when Nick tried to physically confront them. Interesting."

David, overhearing this, stood up, his head shaking back and forth, his voice mirroring the sudden fear on his face. "You don't know. You're jumping to conclusions, you don't know what they're like."

"No," Derek agreed, turning and walking over to stare him down; the tall, craggy-faced man overpowering the more slender figure like a tiger facing down a cheetah. "We do not. All we have is your word on it. No details, no explanations, nothing but a very successful play on our emotions. And that is not enough for me to risk the lives of my people on."

Nick, seeing David tense up, opened his mouth to protest, but Rachel reached out to place a firm hand on his shoulder. When he looked up at her, she shook her head gently, her large dark eyes eloquent. Not now. Not when they needed to present a unified front.

Nick looked back at David, who had retreated back into the comfort of the dark blue upholstered armchair. Hunched like a pouting child, his long straight hair falling into his face as though a shield to hide behind, he was a pitiful sight.

Nick set his jaw. Derek didn't know what he was implying. He couldn't understand. The poor kid was obviously terrified of whatever it was that was out there, and no matter how well they might have read *Miss Manner's Guide to Breaking, Entering, and Assault*, there was no way in hell that Nick was going to play forgive-and-forget.

Shaking off Rachel's hand, he followed David, moving to stand next to the chair. It was a clear message—this is where I stand. Shoulders down, arms relaxed, Nick made sure that his body didn't offer any sign of confrontation. He didn't want to challenge Derek, not when he knew that the man had reasonable doubts, doubts that he, Nick, shared to a certain extent. But he wouldn't leave David feeling like he didn't have a supporter, either.

Damnit, he hated when this happened. His training was to follow orders. His faith in Derek, and his trust in that man's instincts, reinforced that training. But sometimes, you just had to do what you felt was right.

The older man looked at him, and Nick could practically feel the weight of that stare. Not hostile, merely . . . weighing. Judging.

"Nick." Rachel was trying to play the peacemaker again, but Nick couldn't let her. He could feel his back muscles stretch into parade attention, his gaze meeting Derek's evenly.

A gesture, the merest flick of Derek's hand, and Nick squeezed David's shoulder once for reassurance and moved off to a quiet nook on the far side of the library, where they would have privacy for the coming argument.

But, to his surprise, Derek didn't light into him. Instead, the Proctor looked . . . concerned?

"He's not the innocent he would have us believe, Nick."

"I know. And I know he's keeping stuff from us. But the fear's real, Derek. He'd rather die than go back to

124

them, whatever they are. How much more than that do we need to know?"

"Be careful what you wish for," Derek said, then shook his head when Nick would have asked for clarification. "Stay with him, Nick. And if he lets anything slip, however slight—"

"I'll pass it along, yeah, I know, Derek. I'm not getting soft just because I don't agree with you."

"I didn't think you were. But . . . be careful."

Nick nodded, tension he hadn't even been aware of fading from his body, leaving only the usual crisis-induced adrenaline sting to animate his exhausted body. This argument wasn't over, but Derek was giving him room to maneuver.

Room to get David to confide in me. To show Derek that his worry's unfounded. Or—and that's the rub— that he's right.

Leaving Nick to wrestle with his thoughts, Derek walked back to where the others were waiting with various degrees of patience.

"I think we need to test the boundaries of our captivity. Alex, if you would come with me?"

Alex nodded, her dark brown eyes resting on Nick for a moment before she put down her coffee mug and followed Derek out of the library.

Rachel, obviously feeling awkward, stood as well, meeting Nick halfway as he came back toward them. "I'll just . . ." and she gestured toward the Control Room. Nick gave her a smile of thanks that she returned, a faint quirk of her lips, before slipping back into the hidden room.

"Hey, David. Come here. I'm going to need your help with these monitors, okay?"

David lifted his head, took in the fact that the two of them were alone in the library, and blinked. "Um. Okay. What do you want me to do?"

The question gave Nick pause. Unfortunately, there wasn't a great deal David could do. They had already culled most of the usable material from the library's shelves, so putting him back to work there would have been completely useless, and he would have figured that out pretty quickly. The real work right now was in the Control Room, where Rachel was. But that was strictly eyes-only. Derek would have his hide for upholstery, rightfully so, if he let David so much as poke a toe into there again.

Then again, it wasn't necessary for David to be actually physically present for him to access the information there now, was it?

"Thank god for technology," he said.

"What?"

"Hang on for a sec, okay? Just sit here," and he led David to the chair by the bank of computer terminals. "Sit here, and I'll be right back."

David sank into the padded swivel chair and looked around, curious. The Black woman, Alex, had been sitting here earlier, and he had been hesitant to come closer to look. She didn't like him, he could tell, and that made him uneasy. Even more than the delicate-looking blond doctor who poked and prodded and frowned so much. She had a lot of say with Derek, and Nick, he could tell. She could get them to kick him out, and he wasn't ready, yet, to give up this refuge.

But she had gone, and Nick was here, and Nick was on his side. So now he took in every detail, from the keyboard set on a recessed drawer that pulled out and back smoothly, to the satiny grain on the wooden cabinets the monitors were set in. To the intricate detail of the image currently forming and reforming on the screen, a large red script "L" that turned in space, almost three-dimensional.

"It's just a screen saver I programmed." David

126

jumped. He hadn't realized that Nick had returned and was standing right behind him.

"Screen saver?" he asked, trying to get his heart to slow down. It was only Nick, he reminded himself. Nick wasn't going to hurt him. He didn't need to be constantly on guard here.

"Yeah, it protects the screen from image burn, if you leave it on too long."

"Oh." David had no idea what Nick was talking about, but decided to nod anyway.

"Okay, I want you to watch these readouts," and he reached over David's shoulder in order to tap a command on the keyboard. Two of the screens cleared, cutting away to a confusing flow of colors and lines. After David stared at them for a while, the one on the left resolved into a map of some sort, a topographical map, only in 3-D, like the screen saver had been.

"Rachel's redirected the feed from the main terminal to these screens," Nick explained. "This one," and he tapped the top of the right-hand terminal, "is what's going on outside. See the blue swirls here? That's the fog. The green beyond that's not moving is still air. The red lines you see here, and here, that's us. The outlines of our wardings."

"Some of the blue's gotten past the lines," David observed, proud that his voice didn't shake.

"Yeah, we know. So far, it's not gotten inside the actual house. This screen here," and he indicated the one on the left, with the map, "is the geologic display. It's a map of the entire island. Those gradations over there are where our power lines come onshore, and this up here, is us. The darker, smaller rise here and here, those are the security checkpoints. You know, those things you somehow got past?" But a friendly grin took whatever sting there might have been out of his words.

"We've got sensors embedded all over the island, in

the bedrock. They're leftover from some survey the government did a couple of decades ago. Something about earthquake testing, trying to determine if this old heap was going to survive the next big one."

"And will it?"

"Did pretty well in '89, from what I'm told. Okay, here's what I want you to do. Keep an eye on this screen," and he indicated the swirling masses of color. "If anything changes color, or looks weird, or does anything it's not doing right now, check it against the map, and let me know what's happening."

"So you can tell if they're related, the quakes and Them? The fog? But don't we know that already?"

"Proof, my friend. The difference between knowing a thing, and being able to prove it; that's a narrow chasm, but a deep one, to quote an old drill sergeant of mine. And you have to be able to prove a thing before you can solve it."

David blinked again, completely lost at the mathematical reference. So he instead fastened on the one thing Nick had said that made sense to him.

"You were in the military?"

Nick laughed, sitting down next to David and turning on the other monitor, which immediately showed a web of glittering, glowing lines that seemed to have no discernable pattern. "Oh, yeah. Either the best years of my life, or the worst, depending on how you look at it."

David turned to his screen, biting his lower lip. "Yeah. I know that song."

"You want to talk about it?"

"No."

"Okay."

There was a pause, then "I've missed a lot, haven't I? While I was . . . away."

"Oh, just a rash of terrorist attacks on U.S. soil, the return of 70's fashion, major genocide going on over in

Eastern Europe, the bombing of a Federal building by some of our own loonies, O.J. Simpson got away with murder, and a purple dinosaur became the most hated creature in the world."

"Oh." David blinked. "Not much then, huh?"

"Nope. Not much."

In the main entranceway, Derek paused, listening to the faint sound of male voices coming from the library, then continued through the house. It was still, quieter than he could ever remember. Even when most of the team was off elsewhere, there was still an underlying hum of a house that was lived in. Phones rang, doors opened and closed, the furnace occasionally rumbled or, less often, the air conditioning . . . Today, for the first time, it felt empty.

"But it is not. There are people here," he said out loud, although Alex wasn't quite certain who he was reminding—the forces outside, or himself. Another rumble shook the house, as though in answer to his words. "And you don't care, do you?" he asked rhetorically. She looked at him, and refrained from commenting.

Increasing his pace, Derek strode down the hallway until they came to one of the smaller doors leading outside. Alex, who had been forced to stretch her legs just to keep up, almost knocked into him when he stopped suddenly. These doors had been placed after the house had been constructed in order to facilitate getting between the wings of the house. It had cut travel time considerably, a plus in a structure this size.

Through this particular door, you could cut across a narrow courtyard, then go through another door and into an outcropping of rooms they tended to use as a storage area of sorts. Alex bit her lip, remembering only then that she had been planning to clean up in there this week. Another set of good, if mundane, intentions, blasted by

129

unforseen complications. That should be the motto of her life. Welcome to the Legacy.

"All right, Derek. What are we going to do, make a run for it?"

"Something of that sort," he replied, measuring the distance out the window with an appraising glance. Barely dawn, the fog was nonetheless picking up all sorts of weird lighting from within, giving the landscape an eerie glow. "I want you to open the door, thinking about going to the storerooms."

"And once I'm tossed back on my keester, what then?"

"Just do it, Alex. Please?"

Rolling her eyes, she squared her shoulders, shook back her hair, and reached for the doorknob, trying not to brace herself too much against what was going to happen.

Much to her surprise, what happened was that the door opened easily, swinging back to reveal a narrow path in the fog. Just wide enough for her to walk through, just deep enough for her to see the grass underfoot, it led directly to the door on the opposite side of the courtyard.

Surprised, but not completely astonished, she looked back over her shoulder at Derek. "They can read our minds?" Well, why not?

"Intentions, perhaps. Or perhaps it is merely a case of extrapolating our intentions from our actions. Or it might be a trap."

"Gee." Alex grimaced. "Thanks for the encouragement."

But she moved forward nonetheless, the fog swirling impenetrably just inches over her head. Only a few feet to her left, there should have been a line of trees, green branches with the unmistakable scent of pine sap rising through the air. But instead there was only a damp, rusty smell, plus a tang of ozone, as though a lightning bolt had hit metal and burned through the air. But weren't elves allergic to iron?

Alex shook her head, trying to put those thoughts out of her head and concentrate instead on putting one foot in front of the other. Think of the storeroom, Derek had told her. Intentions. My intent is to get to the storeroom without mishap. That's all.

Step, step, step, her sneakers making soft swishing noises as she crushed the dew-wet grass under her feet. And that was the only noise. Even her breathing seemed silent, as though it were holding itself back for fear of rousing some dreadful beast.

"I hate you, Derek Raynes. Like telling someone not to think of elephants . . ."

Despite the clear path in front of her and the damp warmth of the fog, Alex felt a shiver run down her spine. It had nothing to do with the climate and a lot to do with the fact that she was being watched. Turning slightly, she saw Derek still standing in the doorway. But it wasn't his steady concern that made her feel uneasy.

"Hello? Are you out there? We don't mean you any harm."

Nothing answered, and she found herself at the other door without further incident. Opening it, the screen door sticking slightly, she crossed the threshold, then turned to look back at Derek for further instructions.

The fog seemed to press at her, as though urging her inside, but it did not pass the threshhold itself.

"Polite, aren't you? So, it's okay to trash the place, send tendrils of what-have-you poking around, and trap us in here, but you won't come past the doorway. Unless you're invited, I guess, which I'm not doing. So don't get any ideas."

Standing her ground, she watched as tendrils curled

just shy of her skin and backed off again. "Interesting. Maybe they were listening." She looked up again to see Derek leaving the doorway, heading not through the path, toward her, but out into the direction of the fog that should lead out of the courtyard.

"Oh boy. Derek I don't think that's such a good—"

And with a powerful blow that she could feel in her own torso, he was thrown back into the pathway, landing with an audible ooomph.

"—idea. Derek?!"

Standing slowly, he lifted one hand to indicate that he was all right, and she breathed a sigh of relief. Undaunted, he tried to push his way back into the fog, to where the path still ran from one door to another. This time, however, he found himself blocked, as though the mist had suddenly turned to steel everywhere he touched.

Finally giving up, Derek indicated to her that she should return. Swallowing dryly, Alex took a tentative step back across the entranceway. "I'm just going back there, okay?" The fog continued to swirl outside the narrow walkway, curving into elongated fingers, but nothing came out of it to obstruct her.

On a sudden whim, she pushed her fingers into the wall of the walkway. The fog parted reluctantly, as though it were made of pudding. When her palm made contact, however, she felt a cold shock run through her skin, making a cold shiver run through her blood.

"Okay. Okay. I get the message."

"So."

Derek stood in the library again, looking out a window at the fog. As the hours dragged past their pre-dawn wake-up call and into the morning, the sun had begun to filter through the fog. Now they could see that it wasn't a solid block of gray, but rather bands of color, gradations running from pearlized white to metallic shimmers of colors: red, green, blue, orange. That must have been what created the odd glow.

"So you got tossed, too. What did that prove?" Nick asked. Rachel had finally persuaded David to lie down, with the agreement that they wouldn't cut him out of what was happening. As a compromise, a cot had been pulled from storage and set up in the far corner of the room, and Rachel now sat with him there, trying to convince him to try to sleep. Derek looked at them, his eyes dark with unvoiced, uncomfortable thoughts. Had they always spent so much time in here? And if so, why hadn't anyone thought to replace that god-awful wallpaper?

With an effort, he turned his attention back to Nick's question. "Only that I was, as you say, tossed. Alex managed to get from point A to point B without any hindrance. Even after my ill-fated attempt to leave the house's immediate vicinity, she was not hampered."

"So long as I stayed on the path that had been cleared," Alex reminded him. "They wouldn't let me go away from that."

"But it was a reminder, not a punishment. Parental, one might almost say."

"Well . . . yes," the young woman admitted. "I don't know that I would have called it Dr. Spock-approved, but it wasn't painful. More like getting your fingers slapped, if that much."

"Fairies with manners?" Nick's voice was plainly skeptical.

Derek paced away from the window, lowering his voice even more to ensure that it did not carry to David's ears. "As I said before, the faerie realms have always worked within rules of their own. They may be incomprehensible to us, but there is structure."

He paused to take a sip of coffee, then continued.

"There seem to be very clear rules as to what is and what is not allowed in this case as well. Fact: despite a demonstrated ability to damage the structure of the house itself, they have not caused serious damage. Fact: when their intrusions threatened a secure room, where certain items of dangerous supernatural properties are stored, they backed away, implying a reluctance to create more harm. Fact: they have not harmed anyone outside the house and allowed those outside the immediate house boundaries to leave the island unmolested. And fact: when we—those with direct contact with David—attempted to leave the house, we were restrained in a manner that was obviously not designed to injure."

"So what you're saying is . . . what *are* you saying?"

Alex's tone was a perfect mix of curiosity and indignation and brought a faint smile to Derek's face. "I am wondering if these new players see us as threats, as contaminated by David's presence, or perhaps as possible allies. I am beginning to wonder if perhaps we have been making a few erroneous assumptions about the game that is being played here. And if perhaps our young guest has remembered anything more about his captors, and why they are so intent on recapturing him . . . but, apparently, not in taking anyone else."

The three of them turned, almost as though pulled by one string, to look at Rachel and David.

NINE

David blanched. "W-what are you talking about? I've told you everything. I wouldn't lie to you!"

"You might, if you felt it was in your best interest," Derek said calmly. "But I'm more interested in what you haven't told us than what you have. Why, if these Sidhe are so terrifying, haven't they harmed anyone else? Why are they so focused on you?"

"And why haven't they forced their way in yet?" Alex wondered.

David's bravado gave out suddenly, as though his insides had crumpled under the pressure. "They only want me," he said sullenly. "They're not interested in any of you. You don't need them."

"And you did," Rachel said softly. "You wanted them . . . wanted what they had to offer. An end to what? The dreariness of life out here? The responsibility for making decisions?" Her voice wasn't accusing, and he managed to meet her gaze.

"I was an idiot."

"That much we're in agreement on," Nick said, but not without sympathy.

"Anything else you want to share?" Derek asked, shooting Nick a warning glare.

David shook his head. His skin was ashen, and his hands were shaking from the stress.

"Derek, enough. Now that we know we're not in danger—" Rachel was watching their visitor with a worried eye, clearly measuring the distance she'd have to dash were he to collapse.

David interrupted her. "I didn't say that. I said they don't want you. But they want me . . . and you're in the way." His puppy dog eyes touched on each one of them in turn. "If you abandon me, they'll go away. But they'll take me with them. And I'll die there, I swear I will."

And everyone in the room believed him.

Armed with this new information, and a few suppositions of their own, divide and research became the order of the day.

Derek retreated to his personal study, hoping to find something useful in the more esoteric of his research materials, ones he had held off on searching at first, until he was certain that he needed them. Several of the volumes were so old and delicate that they could only be opened in a controlled environment for fear of damaging them beyond repair. Alex had wanted to scan them into the main computer for some time, but Derek so far had resisted.

He didn't like to think he was elitist. But such potentially dangerous information simply shouldn't be available with the ease of a download.

Rachel, in the meantime, had used the distraction as an excuse to cart David off for yet another examination. He managed to rally enough to put up a protest, but

Rachel, concerned about his growing weakness when he should have been getting better, took him by the collar and marched him off.

Even in his sanctum, Derek could hear David's strident protests, all the way down the hallway to where Rachel had set up an office-away-from-the-office.

"If you're a good boy," she promised, "I'll give you a lollypop when we're done."

And then David's voice, fainter now, asked, "Grape?"

With Derek handling the supernatural research side, and Rachel concentrating on their one source of direct— if uncommunicative—information, that left only one other avenue of research to consider. And two members of the team left to follow up on it.

Nick followed Alex down the hall of the guest wing to the room David had been assigned. It was the first room on that short corridor since they—thankfully—had not been expecting anyone else when he arrived. But in that short distance, Nick had managed to vocalize some world-class grumbling not quite under his breath.

"I don't see why we need to toss his dirty laundry. Especially since it's all my clothing anyway. The only thing you'll find in the pockets are—"

"Please," Alex said. "Don't tell me. Let it be a surprise."

He made a "ha-ha" face, pulling the heavy wooden door open and ushering her inside with a mocking flourish. She rolled her eyes at him, amused in spite of herself. He just had that effect on her, even when he was being a pain.

She proceeded past him into the darkened room, turning on the floor lamp just inside the door as she went. "I'd forgotten how dark the house can get. We've had so many sunny days recently, I haven't had to turn on any lights until dusk. Hey, I wonder if it's intentional, if the gloom outside is supposed to be some kind of a psychological weapon, to make us even jumpier or depressed?"

Before following her into the room, Nick snagged the straight-backed chair they had used during their stints of body-watching and used it to prop the door. He wanted to be able to hear if anyone came up the stairs and down the hallway. "Maybe. Would make sense," he said in answer to Alex's question, but his mind was on more immediate matters. Rachel had promised to keep David occupied with a series of tests, both psychological and physical, while they were snooping. But short of tying him to the chair, she couldn't guarantee he wouldn't bolt. And having David show up unexpectedly, catching them in the act, was something Nick wasn't willing to risk. That was a scene that could get . . . unpleasant. Which brought the ex-SEAL back around to his original complaint.

"What do we—excuse me, you—expect to find in here anyway? Some kind of written confession?"

Alex heard under the forced casualness tone of his voice, down to the confusion he was trying to hide. *Poor Nick*, she thought. *This may be too close to home for him . . .*

"Derek," and she emphasized their leader's name, "thinks that there might be some clue to what David's been through, what he's not telling us, in the way he—" She threw up her hands in frustration. "Oh, I don't know, Nick! In the way he folds his damn underwear!"

Nick paused, his irritation washed away by an expression of mock surprise. "Alex, no one folds their underwear!"

When she didn't react, he stopped fiddling with the chair's placement and looked at her. "Alex?"

The raven-haired woman stood just by the bed, one hand palm-flat down on the rumpled coverlet. The pillows were tossed to the foot of the bed, and the sheets were halfway off the mattress. David obviously wasn't much on making his bed. Or any kind of housekeeping, for that matter, based on the clothing and towels tossed around the room.

"Alex?"

No response. She didn't even twitch.

Concerned, he left the doorway and moved across the room in two long strides, grabbing her by the shoulders and pulling her away from the bed.

"Alex!"

Her eyes blinked, then slowly refocused on him. "Nick."

"The one and only. Where'd you go, Alex?"

"I . . . I don't know." She was hesitant, her normally strong voice now sounding as though it came from far away, from a much older and shakier person. "It was so strange . . . like falling down a tunnel. A rabbit hole. It twisted, but it was straight down, too. And I was falling so fast . . . It was totally dark, no lights. I couldn't see a thing, but there were colors, too. And a narrow band of silver; glinting, almost glowing. Painful. God, it hurt!"

She tore away from Nick's concerned grasp, backing up against the bed. Surprised by the impact on the back of her knees, she sat down abruptly on the mattress, her hands going down to balance herself. Her fingers curled into the coverlet, the skin under her nails blanching under the pressure she was inflicting.

Nick started at her sudden movement, prepared to pull her away from the furniture if she fell into a psychic trance again, but her eyes stayed clear, if a little distracted. She was still with him.

He must have made some kind of sound, because she looked up, her expression and voice half embarrassed, half apologetic. "Sorry. I think . . . I think that I got caught up in his thoughts, his emotions—his dreams, maybe, considering the amount of time he's spent sleeping or unconscious in this bed. Confusion, fear—Nick, he's really scared."

"I think this is where I'm supposed to say 'I told you so,' " Nick said wryly, sitting down on the bed next to her. "But I won't."

"Gee, thanks." Her answering smile was equally wry, and he relaxed a little. As often as he saw her or Derek do that, it still spooked him more than a little. It was nice to have some supernatural mojo on their side, but it was still unnerving to someone who liked to have their weapons manifest a little more on the material plane, so to speak.

Another tremor came, but by now they were almost accustomed to it, and it didn't cut into their conversation.

"So, seen enough, or do you still want to delve into his underwear drawer?"

"It's your underwear, you delve," she said. "I'll check out the bathroom, see if he hangs up towels any better than he does his, sorry, *your* clothing."

"Right." He stood up and moved toward the low dresser, which matched the bed frame and chair in design. Not his favorite style, the heavy curlicues and carvings, but it did seem to suit this room, with the old-fashioned textured wallpaper and Tiffany-style light fixtures. As he passed the lamp on the table by the bed, he turned it on, the additional light making a valiant effort to lift some of the gloom the entire house seemed shrouded in today.

Alex also stood. But instead of going into the bathroom, she turned toward the far wall. Several framed black-and-white photographs there failed to catch her attention, despite the stark beauty of the mid-nineteenth-century snowscapes they captured. Instead, her gaze slid

140

to the window, where the pearlized gray of the fog threw back the light in weird shadows.

Unable to hold that sight for very long without feeling distinctly uncomfortable, she looked down to where the cream-on-cream flocked wallpaper met the polished wooden floor. The dark, narrow planks glistened in the pool of light from the lamp and window, drawing attention to the intricate grain of the wood.

Her gaze fogged again, and her mouth opened slightly, as though preparing to ask a question. She shook her head, dispelling whatever was tickling at the back of her mind, and squinted in an attempt to filter out some of the lighting's influence.

"Nick?"

"Mmmm?"

"Come here, look at this, will you?"

His presence at her shoulder was comforting in a solidly practical way. That was Nick: rational and practical and blunt as a clue-by-four. If there was something there, and not just her mind playing tricks, Nick was the person to find it.

"What?"

"Do you see anything? There," and her right hand lifted, pointing. "On the floor."

"Um, wood, some dust—way too much dust, actually. We've got to keep these rooms in better shape. Um, and something sparkling over there. Is that what you meant?" He picked up one of the smaller, more portable lamps and went closer to the wall. Something sparkled under the redirected light, confirming Alex's suspicions.

Placing the lamp on the floor, the better to work by its light, Nick dropped to one denim-clad knee and ran a finger carefully along the molding that joined floor and wall.

"Ow!" was followed by a swear word, bitten off halfway out of his mouth. Alex bent over him, her expressive

141

face creased in concern. "What happened?"

He held up his index finger as though to show her a boo-boo. Even as he did so, a tiny drop of bright red blood formed on the pad of his finger, welling up rapidly.

"Ouchies," he said solemnly, making her giggle as much from relief of tension as anything else. A splinter, in the scheme of things, was so disgustingly normal. He started to put the injured finger in his mouth to suck the blood away, but she caught at his hand, bringing it closer to her face in order to inspect the wound.

"Don't be an idiot. There's something still in there. I think it's—do you have your Swiss Army Knife with you?"

"Always. Didn't I tell you that I was a boy scout? Always prepared, etc., etc." As he spoke, he reached with his free hand down into his front jeans pocket. Pulling out a small version of the instantly-recognizable red pocket knife, he flicked open the tweezer tool and handed it to her.

"Be gentle with me," he requested.

She grinned at that. "Don't tease, Nick. I don't think my heart could take it."

A moment of concentration, her lower lip caught between rows of even white teeth, and she extracted a tiny splinter from his finger. Held up for examination, it glistened faintly in the diffused lamp light.

"Metal," Alex diagnosed. "Some kind of iron shaving, I think."

"We're really going to have to talk to the cleaning staff," Nick deadpanned. "Dust is one thing, but this is nasty."

"This was intentional, Nick."

"The cleaners left metal shavings scattered all over the floor on purpose? *Definitely* going to have to have a talk with them."

"Nick! Metal—iron—cold iron?" When he showed no sudden flash of understanding, she spelled it out for him. "Cold iron is supposed to ward off the supernatural, remember? Specifically, elves."

He looked at his finger, then at the line of glittering dust now obvious along the baseboard, then back at Alex. "David." It wasn't a question.

"David," she said grimly. "Nobody else would have had reason to do it. Which means Derek was right: he *is* hiding something from us. Information that scares him enough to build further protections around his own room—but that he was willing to leave us in the dark about. Leaving *us* in danger."

Nick frowned, standing slowly. "I'm not ready to convict him just yet, Alex. You can't assume that he meant to put us in danger just on the basis of some metal shavings dropped on the floor. Innocent until proven guilty, remember?"

"He's not innocent, Nick." She indicated the evidence on his hand. "He may not be guilty of anything we could call a crime, but he's using us, trying to get us to . . ."

"To what?" Nick demanded.

"I don't know."

His face, so open a moment before, had closed up, erecting a wall between them. "Right. Why don't we ask him before you hire the hangman?"

"Nick, I only meant that—"

But he had turned and left the room.

"Damn." She stood as well, closing the Swiss Army Knife and shoving it into her own pocket. "Well . . . damn."

Part of her wanted to go after Nick, to try to explain her fears, her suspicions. They were friends, first and foremost, and she hated the thought of his anger being directed at her for any reason.

But the problem was that she still didn't know *why*

she felt this way about David. And Nick was right, she had already convicted him based on those feelings. Feelings she had learned over the years to trust implicitly. And if Nick was so caught up in his plan to save David from his demons to the point where he wasn't listening to his coworkers, well . . .

"Then that's the way it has to be." Her eyes narrowed, tracking the lines of metal dust. It was clear now, once you knew what to look for: a thin rivulet of sparkles running along the molding of the floor, then doubling back under the window. She bent down to gather more of the dust, then sat back on her haunches and reconsidered. This wasn't enough to actually keep out anything that could breach their defenses. If it served any purpose at all, it would have been as a beacon, alerting supernatural beings that there was something in this room being hidden from them. So . . . was it actually for protection? And if so, protection from what? What else could it be used for?

"From himself," she said slowly, realization dawning. "He's trying to keep himself from rejoining them, from going outside. But such a thin line, it's only a stopgap measure—he has to have something else that will anchor him here permanently."

Derek carefully replaced the illuminated pages in the document case and closed the glass top. Every time he handled the fragile parchment that was all that was left of Sir Ellis Leithead's *Fey and the Damage to the Christian Soul* he held his breath, certain that the priceless documents were finally going to crumble to dust. But once again, the collection he had spent half a lifetime and a great deal of the Legacy's money acquiring had paid off.

Moving away from the case, Derek returned to his desk and sat down heavily. In his hand was a small notebook with quickly jotted notes, a distillation of the heavily ornate prose Sir Ellis had favored.

"I suppose it could have been worse. It could have been in Latin," he told himself. But there was no humor in his voice. Leithead always left him with a pounding headache just above and behind his left temple. And today had been no different. What he had discovered, rereading a portion of the man's ramblings, had merely confirmed his fears. If Sir Ellis was to be considered at all accurate, that was. But Derek had it on excellent authority that while Leithead might have been considered a certified lunatic by polite society, he was also quite unerringly accurate when it came to his writings on the supernatural.

Placing the notebook on the desk in front of him, his fingers tapped the pages absently, his face set in stern lines that indicated unpleasant thoughts. Another tremor rolled through the house, this one less aggressive than earlier ones. He noted that they were becoming more selective, as though searching for fault lines that would bypass the areas of danger within the house itself. But not so selective that they weren't doing damage to the rest of the house, he thought, hearing the faint thud of something heavy falling to the floor above him.

"I hope that was furniture and not a person." He tilted his head in the manner of an inquisitive dog, listening for any further sounds that might indicate damage to a living being. But there was only silence.

Reassured somewhat, Derek put everything going on outside the room out of his mind and refocused his attention on the job at hand. If these tremors were not going to break the building open in one blast or weasle in along existing faults, then they could only be distractions. And if they were meant to be distracted, it must mean that a way to ward off their assailants was here, somewhere within their grasp. They need only find it. And recognize it.

Flipping the notebook open, he studied phrases at random, trying to let his surface brain come up with a different interpretation. But the words still said the same thing, over and over and over.

If a mortal man transcribes the faery veil, be warned, for his mind will be clouded with such confusion as to render him insensate. And so he shall remain for a span of time, for such is the cost of consorting with those godless, soulless creatures common folk term the fey or Good Neighbors, of which they are indeed not.

Derek made a note on a fresh piece of paper. Confusion, probable mental dislocation, possibly from crossing over the demarcation between mortal and Faerie planes. So far, so accurate. No way to know. But with David as a test subject, Rachel could do up a very nice paper on the effects of faery border-markers on the memory functions of the brain.

Somehow, though, I can't see the Lancet *publishing it.* The Journal of Mythology and Medicology, *perhaps. If they ever recovered their funding after the recent budget cuts.*

Continuing to read, he idly sketched a crude triangle in the margin of his notes, shading the structure in to create a three-dimensional effect. Human in one corner, faery in another, and David the third point, with the Legacy making up the fourth side of the triangle, the base keeping them all apart. How would one detect these lines of demarcation? Were they possible to avoid, or were mortals forever doomed to blunder across them? Or was it selective, the residents needing to unlock the door before an outsider might come in? Which legend was based in fact, and which in wish and dream and fear?

He skimmed the rest of his notes, his body slumping

a little, perhaps in an unconscious attempt to protect his back from the menace he could feel creeping up on him. Although the specifics were never addressed, Leithead wrote like someone who had personal encounters with Faeries, and unpleasant ones at that. It was a shame, really. Derek admitted to himself that, in the midst of all his training, and despite his own experiences, he carried the faintest wish that there was somewhere the simple, mischievous, or even benevolent creatures so beloved by popular culture. Surely not all supernatural creatures stood in the darkness. Couldn't they, like humans, have a range of inclinations, from evil to good?

"Clap your hands if you believe," he said softly, then exhaled through his nose and shook his head, amused at himself. Spend any time reading the original sources and even the most innocuous woodland sprite showed a darker origin. And the outrightly malevolent figures far outweighed any helpful brownie or hobgoblin.

A man might admire their pale beauties, Leithead wrote, *but he does so at the risk of his immortal soul. For they are spiteful creatures which cannot bear the Lord's Grace to fall on another, and so will spirit away those who espy them, and torment them until they cast off all claims of Redemption.*

Again, this tied in with what David had told them, that he had been taken in and held captive, escaping only through luck and desperation. That only his long association with the fey folk had allowed him to find the points where one might cross back into the mortal world. But somehow, it just didn't sit right. Not false, but not exactly true, either.

Like everything else about David.

"You're going on gut feeling," he warned himself, tapping the tip of his pencil against his drawing. "Back it up. Prove you're not just reacting this way because his 'poor little lost me' act rubs you the wrong way. Or you won't be in any position to refute Nick when he rides in as David's champion."

In truth, the glamour of these beings is of such ungodly strength that none but a man with strong will might ever recover, and that only if he be of such pious nature to ward off their dire influence. For only with the help of the Almighty may a mortal erase Their vile stain from his mind and soul.

Derek stilled his pencil at that. Whatever else might be said of their young guest, pious was probably not one of the words that would first come to mind. Stubborn, yes. Willful, of a certainty. Was a strong will, honed by years of slavery, enough?

"Yes." Derek drew the word out, almost tasting it. "Yes, it would be, if combined with the drive to escape, the desire to survive. And David is a survivor. I would lay good money on that fact." If not, he would have given in to the enchantments of Faerie, would never have attempted escape, much less succeeded.

And yet, both he and Alex sensed something off about the young man, above and beyond the taint of the supernatural that understandably clung to him. Something that made them second-guess his avowals of honesty. That suggested he had not been completely honest with them, that he still held back information.

But why? And—and this was the $100,000 question—what information?

And would not knowing it put the Legacy in worse danger than they already were?

TEN

"**I**'m telling you, I don't remember how I got there! I don't want to remember anything about Them!" David was seated again in the new reading chair, but the comfort was clearly lost on him now. His face was splotched with tears and anger, his eyes red-rimmed. And where just a day before his face had been baby-soft, now it was worn and lined, showing signs of stress and dissipation. The seven years he had lost were coming home to roost, all at once. His voice was scratched and broken, but his back was still poker-straight, refusing to relax into the upholstered embrace of the chair.

Rachel hung back at the edge of the room, her attention split between David and Nick. One part of her mind was watching her patient, noting the sweat beading along his face, the slight tremor in his limbs, ready to step in and stop this if needed. But the rest of her attention was focused on Nick. She placed a gentle hand on his arm, feeling the tension screaming from every muscle in his body. A day's growth on his face hid lines of exhaustion and concern. *I hate this*, she thought. *Why must caring take such a terrible toll?*

Nick clearly wanted to wade in, a bear defending its cub. But, in reluctant obedience to Derek's command, he stayed out of the interrogation.

And it *was* an interrogation. Gone was the kind, almost fatherly expression Derek showed to the majority of the world. Now his brow was creased in anger, not compassion, and his eyes were cold slate that allowed no access to his inner thoughts. If there was one thing Derek Rayne did not handle well, it was being manipulated, being played for a fool. And, based on what he had learned, and Alex and Nick had discovered, that was exactly what David Carson had done.

Derek knew that he could have accepted that. Could have made allowances for David trying to get home, trying to recover something close to normality. He could even have accepted the desperate attempts to lay claim on their sympathy; if emotional ties to someone mortal were what David needed in order to remain here, it only made sense. And hadn't Derek been trying for the same thing, in a way, by putting him and Nick together?

But by omitting facts, by forcing them to work with less than complete information, David had endangered the people in Derek's care. Had, in fact, made targets of them, by flaunting his location in the manner he had. And that—that carelessness for those around him—was unforgivable.

It also raised an interesting question. How could such carelessness translate into a bond strong enough to hold him here?

No time, Derek told himself. Worry about it later. If David expected that thin line of cold iron to be enough to hold him until whatever long-term solution he was planning took over, they didn't have any more time.

They had to know about the Sidhe's hold on him and what their part in this game was.

"I will ask you one last time. How did you come to be in the company of the beings outside? What claim do they have on you?"

"They don't have any claim! I'm not their slave! They don't own me!"

"What is your value to them? Why are they pursuing you with such vehemence?"

"I don't know!"

David drew in a gasping breath, sucking watery snot like a four-year-old. His skin was ashen, his arms trembling where they clenched the side of the chair compulsively. Rachel's concerns were valid. Despite his apparent health when he arrived, there was something terribly wrong with him now. There hadn't been time for Rachel to do more than brief Derek on what her most recent exam had shown, but even that quick rundown had been sobering.

Derek felt his resolve quaver, and firmed it again. This charade had to end, one way or the other. They had to know what had bound David to his captors in order to find the trigger which freed him. And if what he suspected about David's intentions was true, this was the only way to do it. He only hoped that Nick would work with him on this. The discoveries had come so swiftly, the sense of urgency building against his senses with every moment the fog pressed in on them, that there had been no chance to talk to him privately, to try to explain what he was going to do. He would just have to wing it, hope that Nick would pick up his cues when the time came.

"You lied to us. You asked for our aid, invoked our sympathy, caused us to place ourselves in jeopardy, and it was all a lie. Wasn't it?"

"No! No, damn it! Everything I told you was true!"

"But it wasn't the whole truth, was it David?" Alex's voice by comparison was sweet, soft, compassionate. "You kept things from us. Told us you couldn't remember. But you did, didn't you? That's why you warded your room," and she held up a handful of the metal dust they had brought with them, letting it fall slowly to the carpet. "That's why you've been pushing us, trying to get us to take action against them. So that you wouldn't have to face the fact that you don't want to be free. That you *want* to go back to them."

"No!" His denial was a physical scream of agony, his body shaking with repressed truth. But a quick glance up showed no sympathy in Alex or Derek's eyes, and his one ally, Nick, was standing aside, his face averted. "I don't want to go back. Never. I couldn't bear it." He stopped, swallowed heavily, then looked up at Derek with a stark light of hopelessness on his face. "And I didn't lie. I couldn't remember. Not at first. And then only what I told you."

"I don't buy that," Alex said. "I think you remembered everything when you saw the fog. Rachel told us how you reacted to it, to seeing it. Them. Waiting for you. She thought you were afraid. But it wasn't just fear—it was desire."

It was as though someone had punched him in the gut with a pile driver. The defiance went out of him, not in a great huff, but in a slow, silent exhalation. He looked up at the nearest window, almost a reflex action, checking the fog the way an antelope might scent a tiger stalking, both aware of its presence and aware that nothing would deflect its eventual strike.

"You lied to us, even tried to deflect the truth under hypnosis, didn't you," Derek said. "You wanted to keep us in the dark about what was really going on. Why?"

Drawing a deep breath in, David nodded a slow assent. "Yes." His voice was barely a whisper, directed toward his lap. If his repentance was an act, it was a good one. "Seeing them like that, all around . . . then I remembered. I remembered everything. And I knew what they would do to me if they got in. If I let them in. I couldn't . . . I was afraid if you knew, knew what they were, you would throw me out. *I* would have thrown me out. But I wasn't strong enough to deny them on my own."

"And you think that this justifies your actions?" Despite his stance of disinterest, Nick had been following the conversation with growing indignation. But his outburst was directed against David now, the fragile bond the two had forged cracking under these new revelations. "You used us. Used us to do what you didn't have the balls to do for yourself. And you didn't even have the decency to be honest about it. To let us know what dangers we might be in, so we could take precautions. Your selfishness could have cost people their lives!"

David looked up from contemplation of his knees and opened his mouth to say something. But nothing came out.

"Nick, not now," Rachel warned. "You're too close. Let Derek and Alex handle this."

Derek glanced at Nick, saw that Rachel had him well in hand, and turned his attention back to the young— not so young—man seated in front of him.

"Why have they followed you, David? What did you do to tie yourself to them? Why is their hold on you so strong?"

When David, stinging from Nick's verbal assault, clammed up again, Alex placed a sheaf of papers on the table in front of her. It was the report she had compiled before the connection to the mainland died. David's gaze slipped from Derek's face to the papers, then back up again.

"David Carson. Seven years ago, according to the few

records we've been able to find, you were living on the streets, cadging handouts. Treated in a detox center a couple of times, but never quite kicked the habit. Notes here say that you probably weren't trying too hard."

"A junkie," Nick said, his voice thick with disgust. While he might eventually have been willing to excuse David's self-centered actions as a survival mechanism—unpleasant but understandable, in the circumstances—the thought of allowing something like that to take over your life so completely revolted him. Which was precisely why Derek had asked Rachel to keep that one detail from him. Better to have Nick believe that David was looking for a way off the streets, looking for help, rather than giving in. But now that the truth was out, there was nothing to do but hope that Nick's greatheartedness would come through once again, that he would not let himself be distracted.

"The medical records were pretty clear—someone was taking remarkably good notes for a free clinic. I think they were expecting to have to identify the body sometime soon," Rachel added, picking up her part. "Your health was bad, your veins were collapsing, you had a chronic cough, severe scar tissue on your arms and ankles." She shook her head, impressed despite herself at the damage he had managed to do. "In short, you were in lousy shape. Now . . . you arrive on our doorstep with the scars long-healed, and nothing in your veins but blood. A body in perfect health, well enough to swim from the mainland."

Not quite perfect, Derek thought. According to Rachel's exam, the damage was reemerging at an alarming rate, adding to the urgency of the situation. Whatever the Sidhe had done to restore him, it had been a patch, not a cure. The addiction still lurked within his body, in a kind of stasis that had been broken, most likely when he returned to this world. Within a week, Rachel had

154

warned, they might have a full-fledged junkie in withdrawal on their hands.

"They've been taking good care of you, David. So why did you run?"

David's face twisted into a fierce mask, hatred shining through the innocent exterior and finally destroying any lingering glamor of youth. "Good care of me? Good care?" The bitterness in his voice could have curdled sugar. "I was a pet. No, a slave. Their court jester, with bells around my wrists and ankles, and a golden collar around my neck. Dancing for my meals. Being the butt of their jokes, their playtoy, their animal. Is that what you consider good care?"

He tried to get up and was wracked with a sudden spasm that bent him forward. Rachel jumped foward, but he waved her off.

"Don't bother." He straightened slowly, resting his head against the back of the chair a moment, then looking forward to stare Nick straight in the eyes. "You want to know what they are, what they did to me? I'll tell you. Yeah. I was in lousy shape. Seven years ago I shoved everything I could find into my veins, up my nose, into my lungs." He stopped, closed his eyes. "Don't you judge me. Don't you dare judge me!" His voice rose, squeaking a little under the weight of his passion. "You don't know, unless you've been there. It's so sweet at first. And then . . . And then you'll take anything to get through the day, through the night. I lost my job, got kicked out of my apartment, didn't give a damn until I woke up one morning and couldn't remember the last time I had eaten, the last time I had bathed— nothing.

" I tried to get away, tried to stop. Tried to get back to someplace that made sense. But everything hurt, all the time. My body, my brain. Only the junk made it better."

"And they offered to make it all go away? The pain, the confusion." Rachel was soft-voiced now, understanding and forgiving. Her own past hadn't been so squeaky-clean. She knew the desire to make the bad parts disappear, wiped clean as though by magic—or by magic in fact. And that knowing came through and somehow managed to reach David despite his growing hysteria.

The others held their breath, afraid that one wrong sound would make David shut down again.

"She came to me one night." He closed his eyes, and his voice became ruminative, the bitterness fading under the sweetness of memory. His voice became lyrical, poetic, and for a moment they could again see the boy he had once been. "Out of the shadows, she was wrapped in darkness. Tall, glowing with the magic of the moon. A faerie queen, lovely as a shining blade. Her voice sang to me. Seduced me. Oh, I knew she was dangerous, more dangerous than anything I had ever done to myself before. But I didn't care."

His face hardened, wrapped itself in a facade of blandness once again. "I wasn't looking for an end to the pain, Rachel. I was looking for an end, period. I thought that was what she would give me."

"And what did you have to give in return?" Alex asked.

"Nothing. Just agree to go with her, willingly. To do as she asked." He laughed, bitter again. "But she lied to me. They all lied to me."

"The way you lied to us?" Nick's voice, hard and demanding, hiding his disappointment in his new friend. Derek winced, then narrowed his eyes at the two men.

"No!" David exploded from his chair, lurching forward to get directly in the other man's face. "It's not the same at all."

"It is in my book." And Nick deliberately turned

156

away, facing the wall of books instead. Withdrawing the one last support David was resting on. Derek relaxed, mentally congratulating Nick on sapping David's defenses so effectively. Whether he had caught Derek's cue or was merely reacting to the stimuli tossed at him didn't matter, so long as it created the same effect: David's loss of refuge. Oh, there was no doubt that the young man was genuinely angry with their guest. But Nick was channeling that anger into something useful. Something that might in the end save them all, David included.

"What did you agree to, David?" Derek gentled his voice, trying to bring his Sight to bear on the young man. But his gift, as always, would not be commanded.

David looked once at Nick's back, then closed his eyes and turned away himself, instead facing the older man like a soldier facing execution. "Like I said. I agreed to give myself willingly into their care. To be a guest at their table, a friend within their door. To not question, but to obey their rules, their borders." He recited the words, as though they were learned by rote, or burned so deeply into his brain that even his recent trauma hadn't been able to erase it.

"And in return? What did they offer you in return for this obedience?" Derek was insistent, demanding a response. It may not have been fair, and it certainly wasn't kind to do this to the boy, who was so obviously emotionally fragile, but they needed every last detail David could provide.

With that information, the Legacy could make a fair start at freeing David—and themselves—from the force outside. Hopefully.

"An end to the pain. An end to the need. They would make me whole again." He sat down again, this time sinking into the chair as though he were one hundred years old and two hundred years tired. "So damned beautiful. Enchantment." He laughed, a bark of sound. "That word's got no truth to it, once you've seen them dancing. You can't imagine what it was like. You should be thankful you can't imagine."

He closed his eyes. "But they lied. It was all lies. They took advantage of me, of the fact that I couldn't tell what was real from the hallucinations. They were never what they said they were, never were going to give what they promised me."

"What happened? What changed?"

"She changed. Ashanon. My lady. My owner. She brought me over, taught me to see the lands through different eyes. But then she laughed at me, laughed! God, I had no shame where she was concerned. I crawled, on my knees, begging her to take me back. But she sent me away. Said she was tired of me. Tired of my mortal face and my pitiful jestering."

"You fell in love." Nick had moved to stand beside him, his presence comforting now rather than condemning. "But she was faerie. She could never love you that way. Almost all the stories agree on that."

"This wasn't a story!" More softly. "This was my life."

"And so . . . you ran away?" Rachel moved closer as well, her hands warm and healing on his shoulders. "Came home?"

"I tried. First, I simply tried to leave their Court, where Ash and her followers had their parties, their endless parades of music and dancing. But they wouldn't let me. Even when they didn't want me, they held on. I was theirs, their possession. That was when they chained me. Silver links, from wrist to foot, and those damn hounds to watch me whenever I left their rooms. But it was pride, pride only that made them want me. Want to keep me, like a trophy.

"After a while, I wasn't even brought in to be shown

158

off in front of them at their tables. They forgot about me. But the chains remained. And the hounds, those damn hounds . . ."

He broke down in tears then, a horrible dry heaving that wracked his body. Rachel bent down and placed her arms around him, shooting a stern look at Derek, who backed off under it.

"Come on, David. Enough. You've been through enough. No more questions tonight. Back to bed for you, and rest."

He held himself stiffly in her embrace, anxious. "You won't, you won't send me away? Won't give me back over to them?"

They both looked up at Derek, who shifted uncomfortably, aware of all four sets of eyes now upon him, demanding a response, one way or the other.

"I won't make any decisions tonight," he said finally. "We need to discuss this further."

And with that, David had to be reassured.

"I can't believe you just let him walk out of here."

"Where do you think he's going to go, Alex?" Derek collapsed into the newly-vacated chair before Alex could claim it. "He cannot leave the house any more than we can. Less so, in fact. He has made himself a captive here as much as he was there. Why should we inflict more useless penalties? Merely to make ourselves feel better?"

Alex took a deep breath, obviously gathering patience from some deep, tapped-out well. "No. Of course not." But the words seemed dragged out of her, not an acquiescence given willingly.

"I realize that you are angry. I am as well. But it serves no purpose now. What we have to face now is that a decision must be made. What are we going to do with our young guest?"

He looked up at Alex, standing before him, then over

to where Nick was still leaning against the wall. "Nick? You have been rather silent."

"Unusual for me, huh?" But the usual ironic humor was missing from his voice. Refusing David, even for that short period of time, had drained him. "I don't know, Derek. I just . . . He isn't a boy scout, that's for certain. But he's been hurt so badly. Those scars on his back might have been from when he was on the street, since time apparently got wonky for him, but maybe not. Maybe they wailed on him pretty good, with their little faery sticks and stones."

"It's possible," Derek allowed. "Rachel said that the scars looked to be several years old, but that was before we realized that we were dealing with a temporal displacement as well. Anything is possible. In addition to the return of drug-induced damage to his system, we should be seeing general aging as well, although not quite as swiftly."

"So, the question remains," Nick said, sitting on the very edge of the low table and scuffing the soles of his shoes against the carpeting. "How can we not help him? That's what we do, right? Help humans against supernatural forces?" His lips twisted in a wry smile, and he rubbed at his cheek with the back of one hand. "Well, one human, one supernatural force obviously arrayed against us—it should be a pretty simple military equation, right?"

He looked first at Derek, then at Alex. "Only this is less military, and more politics. We're not talking a war, we're looking at a . . . at a treaty, I guess. And a pretty complicated one at that." He paused, dropping his hand abruptly. "I hate politics."

Alex snorted, a surprisingly elegant expression of distaste. "He made his bed, and now he doesn't want to lie in it. Tough. I don't feel like risking my life or the life of anyone else on the word of some ex-junkie oathbreaker who can't face up to what he's done."

"Alex—"

"No, Derek. I won't back down. You asked for our opinions, well I'm giving it to you. I say we shove him out the door and wipe the dust from our hands."

Her black eyes could have ignited forest fires, the anger in them was so intense. Derek was slightly taken aback. He normally would have expected this reaction from the ex-SEAL, who had a tendency to hair-trigger reactions on the questions of honor and loyalty. But Alex . . .

"What, Alex? What is hitting you so hard here? Talk to me. Tell me what you're feeling."

The psychic made an exasperated face, one hand tugging at her curls, and the anger died down a little, enough for her to focus her mirror-bright mind on the problem at hand. "I don't know, Derek. I wish I could point to something and say, here it is, this is what's wrong. But I can't. I just don't like what I'm picking up from him. I never have."

"That's it? You're saying toss him to the wolves, just because you're getting bad vibes again?" Nick retorted, his Galahad tendency rising to the fore again now that the shock of David's past indiscretions had ebbed somewhat.

Derek held up a hand to halt Nick's outburst, but Alex was able to take care of her own defense. Whirling on her fellow Legacy member and good friend, she gave as good as she was getting. "Those vibes have been enough for you, on occasion. You don't seem to mind them when they agree with what you're thinking. And, for your information, I never liked David, never liked what he brought into this house. But I gave him the benefit of the doubt. Let other people's opinions sway me. And you see what's come out of that."

"Oh, so now all of a sudden this is my fault? I don't think—"

"Nick! Alex! Please."

The two drew apart, suddenly aware of the fact that they had been shouting.

Derek had stood, ready to move between them physically should it prove necessary. But upon seeing them forcibly calm themselves, he sat back down in his chair.

"Both of you have valid points. David is, in many ways, a victim. And we can all empathize with his desire to be free, to return to a world of his own, even if it is one that has not treated him well in the past. And in light of that treatment, and what occurred to him on that other world, his lying to us now is a bit more understandable, if still not forgivable.

"But I have a great deal of faith in Alex's 'vibes,' as do you, Nick, if you will calm down enough to admit it. And if she feels that he is even now hiding more from us, or that he is a danger in some way we cannot protect against, then I am inclined to believe her.

"And there is yet a third thing to consider." He glanced at the monitor, which currently showed a cool blue security readout, indicating an all-clear.

"While we have been arguing this—in fact, since the moment we brought David to this room for questioning—there have been no further attacks upon the house."

"They're waiting to see what we decide to do?" Alex was diverted from her ire momentarily, mentally calculating the implications of that.

"Perhaps. And, if they are willing to give us that breathing space, then I suggest we make use of it. To bed, and get some sleep."

"But Derek—"

"No," he cut off Nick's protests. "Sleep. None of us is thinking clearly. Tomorrow will be enough time to make decisions."

"But—"

"No, Nick. We've all gotten wound up over this. We are reacting, letting our emotions dictate our actions."

"And this is different how?" Alex asked, as always finding a smidgen of humor in Derek's lecture. The four of them, Nick and she, Derek and Rachel, had a tendency to lead with their hearts instead of their heads. Especially in cases like this, it was what made them so often effective. But it could also be a handicap.

"Exactly." He refused to bend, seeing that the other man still was not convinced. "Nick, need I remind you of the last time you championed a soul who came to us in need?"

Nick bit back a retort, his expression changing ever-so-slightly from frustration to a pained regret. The entire incident with Emma Scott still stung. She had seemed so terribly in need of their help, a woman running in fear for her life. But she had in fact been a lost soul long before she came to them, and in the end, they had been unable to help her.

"That's not the case here," he said, his jaw firming in a way that both Derek and Alex recognized. "This isn't the same at all."

"I hope that you are correct," Derek said. "For all our sakes."

Upstairs, Rachel had gotten David safely to his room. Now she sat on the bed, folding and refolding a sweatshirt, listening to the sounds of him using the bathroom. The hiss of water in the shower—her orders, to wash the tension from his muscles and the sweat from his skin—stopped, and the shower door opened with a clang. A moment or two of silence, then the flush of a toilet made her smile involuntarily. How long had he gone without those amenities? And yet he had returned to them with alacrity, even requesting a toothbrush.

She frowned. They spent so much time worrying about the big events, moving from one crisis to another, they never thought much about the smaller details. Like what elves might use instead of toothbrushes. Or if they even needed to worry about decay. David's teeth, like the rest of him, were in excellent shape. Did supernatural beings have tartar?

Those thoughts alerted Rachel that she was on the far side of being punchy. What little sleep she had been getting had done nothing to refresh her. In fact, she had woken up this morning more exhausted than when she had crawled into bed.

And if *she* was this wiped out . . . She put down the sweatshirt and stood up, looking around the door frame into the bathroom. Sure enough, David was out on his feet. Awake, yes, wearing the gray flannel pajama bottoms Nick had dredged up from somewhere, staring into the mirror as he moved the toothbrush up and down over Osmond-quality teeth, but the lights were off and there wasn't anybody home inside.

"Come on, you. Get into bed."

"I don' need t'b' tuck'd in," he protested almost incoherently around a mouthful of foaming paste.

"Sure you don't," she said agreeably, moving forward to take him by one elbow. "Rinse and spit."

He rinsed, spat, and turned to give her a "satisfied now?" look.

"Good boy." He might have led them all into danger, he might have been manipulating them from the moment he arrived, but right now he was stirring every single mothering instinct Rachel Corrigan had been blessed with. And that was a formidable force to be reckoned with, as Kat could have told him.

Tugging on his arm, she led him back to the bedroom. Pointing him toward the bed, she watched with satisfaction as he pulled the sheets back and crawled underneath them. He hadn't washed his hair, only slicked it back. Reaching down, she tucked one damp strand behind his ear and studied his face.

"What?"

"Hang on," she said, and went back into the bathroom. There was the sound of water running, and then she came back into the room, turning the bathroom light off behind her.

"Here. Take these." She handed him a glass of water and two small pills.

"Don' wanna—"

"David. Please. I know that you didn't sleep much last night, and I can understand that. Believe me, I understand. You're feeling pretty beat up and not really fond of anyone in this house, and what's going on outside is enough to keep anyone staring at the ceiling all night. But you need to rest, not just your body but your mind as well. These are just something to help you relax enough to stay asleep. Don't worry, they're not really sleeping pills, per se. Just some organics. Alex swears by them when she has a migraine."

Rachel smiled at him engagingly. "Come on. Take them, okay?"

Nodding in grudging agreement, he reached out and took the pills and water. "Okay. But only 'cause you asked nicely." He regarded the pills dubiously, then popped them into his mouth, took a large mouthful of water, and swallowed.

"Good," Rachel said, taking the glass from him and placing it on the table next to the bed. "Now, just lie back and relax. And the only dreams you'll remember will be good ones. I promise."

She smiled at him one more time, then turned out the light and shut the door behind her.

David lay there, the covers pulled up to his chin. A moment passed, then another. The house made a groaning, settling noise as people on the floor below walked about, and the wind—or maybe not the wind—slipped and slithered against the stone walls. He counted to one hundred in his head, then he sat up, spitting the pills into his hand, grimacing a little at the taste.

Once, a long time ago, he would have taken the pills, swallowed them and only hoped for good dreams to carry him away. But after that little scene downstairs, he was supposed to allow her to drug him while they decided his future? No. Not David. He might have done some seriously dumb things in his past, but that was over. Gone. No more waiting for others to make things go right. From now on, he was the one in control.

Tossing the covers aside, he slid out of bed and, moving with deliberate silence, went to the window, which was still covered by the blind he had pulled down the night before. His hand shaking obviously even in the dark, he reached out and raised the shade, slowly. He would show them that he could resist, that he wasn't going to go skipping back into bondage all that easily any more.

The fog swirled, unrelenting. And then, as though slowly realizing that the barrier of cold metal was gone, out of the soft grays something solid gathered. As he watched, entranced, a face began to coalesce; pearly-white skin drawn over impossible cheekbones, wide, overlarge eyes of deepest amber set under waves of blue-black hair falling in disarray.

The face might have seemed human, but the eyes were purely otherworldly. Filled with the moon reflecting on water, the imitation stars glimmering colors. Implacable, without mercy, they still managed to convey a sense of regret, of sorrow at things inevitable, of things once set in motion, impossible to avoid.

David raised his still-shaking hand and placed it against the glass where the face rested. The barest touch, fingertips ghosting along cold glass. "Ashanon . . ."

And then, with a sharp motion that broke the moment, he pulled the shade against the vision once again.

So much for control, he thought bitterly, but with a touch of self-abusing humor. So much for forming ties somewhere else, with someone else. She still owned him. Body. Mind. Soul . . . And heart.

Downstairs in the library, Derek gave up on the book he had been studying, realizing that his notes had deteriorated into near indecipherable scribblings. "I'm getting old. A few years ago, I could have gone for days with only a few hours of sleep."

He pursed his lips, then grinned wryly. "Well, perhaps more than a few years ago. In college, certainly."

Hoping against hope, he lifted the receiver of the phone, but once again, only static greeted his ear. Power ran to the island without interruption, fueling the lights and electricity, but communications were at a standstill, even cell phones.

For himself, were the situation not so dire, it would be a pleasant change, and Nick seemed to be taking it in stride. But Alex was about to start sending out carrier pigeons if she couldn't access her e-mail soon. And Rachel, although she was hiding it well, had to be worried about her daughter. Katherine had been through so much already in her young life; despite a maturity level adults might envy, she still needed to hear her mother's voice when they were separated for more than a day or two.

"This can't go on much longer."

"You got that right."

Turning around in his chair, Derek looked at the newcomer in surprise. "Nick. I didn't hear you come in. I thought you had gone to bed."

"No, you told me to. I never agreed."

Something in the younger man's tone of voice put

Derek on his guard. Not because he thought the younger man was still irritated. His body language, as he stood there, told Derek that the flare-up of temper earlier that evening had died down, as Derek had known it would. Nick didn't hold on to his anger, not against friends. But that didn't mean that all was forgiven.

Derek made a "please continue" gesture, and Nick came around to stand on the other side of the table, looking down across the wooden surface at him. The ex-SEAL's face was shadowed, even under the direct lighting coming from above, but his dark eyes met Derek's without hesitation. And in those eyes, the Precept of the Legacy House could read a colder emotion, like an icy stream running just under the surface.

"You set me up."

Derek respected him too much to prevaricate. "Yes," he admitted simply, pushing back from the table and resting his hands flat against his thighs, waiting for the storm to break.

"*Damn* you, Derek." His well-muscled body tensed, drawing in on itself like a hunting cat about to spring. Had it been anyone else facing him, Nick probably would have lunged across the barrier of polished wood between them, taken his frustration and resentment out in a physical attack. But this was Derek, who never did anything without a reason. Who would never have used Nick's personal demons like that if there had been any other choice. Or so Nick had to believe in order to get through this confrontation.

"You wanted me to bond with him, use my history to win his trust. And then you asked me to betray him." His voice sharpened with disgust, mostly directed inward at himself. "And I did."

"If he had been telling the truth, there would have been no need for betrayal."

"But you knew he wasn't, didn't you? You knew he

was just a selfish, self-serving little ... So it was all okay. But what if you were wrong, Derek? What if, just once, the all-knowing Derek Rayne was *wrong?*"

Derek refused to turn away from that burning gaze. "No matter what David may or may not have done, no matter what lies he told us, your instincts were correct on one very important point. He was in need of a friend."

"Yeah. Some friend. I turned on him."

"Have you?" And now it was Derek's gaze which held Nick frozen in place. Time to get to what was really bothering Nick. "Or have you just proven how valuable your friendship is?"

"Want to run that by me again? How the hell—"

"He lied to us. Endangered everyone on this island without thinking. But you still defend him, protect him, still try to help him out of the shadows he has wrapped himself in. You may not be pleased with him, or like the things he has done in the name of selfishness, but still you hope for the best. If you didn't, you would not be so disappointed in him now. To me, that is friendship of a true and rare sort."

"Yeah. Well, somehow I don't think David sees it quite like that."

"No, I imagine he doesn't. His perception—or lack thereof—does not change the truth, however. Does it?"

The tension in Nick's body finally found expression, turning and stalking away from Derek. But he only got as far as the door when he stopped. He touched the door frame, running his hand along the smooth wood as though looking for an answer, then turned again to look at the older man.

"I'm sorry. I made accusations—"

"That were true." Derek wasn't apologizing, merely stating facts. "I did use you in order to win David's trust. No one else could have gotten that close that quickly.

169

He would have sensed hesitation, suspicion, just as he sensed your compassion." Derek's face softened into sympathy he had not allowed himself to show before. "Whatever else he may or may not have done, Nick, David has been hurt, badly. Both physically and emotionally. And it may be that your friendship is the one thing which has allowed him to open up to us as much as he has. The one chance we have to tie him to this world."

"So the end justifies the means, Derek? Is that what you're saying?"

"I am saying," and he paused. "I am saying that you did nothing that you would not have done purely on your own initiative. And that it was a good thing."

Nick frowned, then nodded abruptly and left the room. Derek sighed again, one hand rising to rub his temples. He had not been prepared for that. Not that he ever could have been. The sharpest instruments could cut the hand that wielded them as surely as they did the object they were set to, and Nick was a very sharp blade. But hopefully, Nick would think about what he had said. Think, and not brood.

The older man snorted. Slim chance of that. Nick was in serious contention for the title of West Coast champion of brood.

Rising, Derek left the library and walked the dark, silent halls toward the kitchen. He could have turned on the lights as he went, but somehow the darkness suited his mood. The fog cast its weird lambent glow, reflecting off the tiling and countertops. In another situation, under different conditions, he would have found it quite restful in an odd sort of way. Like the lack of communication to the outside, it created the feeling of total isolation, a situation that modern man could never really achieve, not in today's world of instant everything.

Opening the fridge, he pulled out a carton of milk,

shook it once to ascertain if there was anything left, then opened the container and sniffed to reassure himself that it had not gone bad. Placing it on the counter, he pulled down a mug from the cabinet and filled it with the cold liquid. Realizing that the refrigerator door was still open, he reached out with one hand to close it.

In the darkness, he lifted the mug with the other and took a sip, sighing as the flavor reached his exhaustion-stale tastebuds. Normally he despised milk except as an accompaniment to his coffee. But tonight, it tasted like manna fresh from the heavens.

Turning away from the fridge, mug in hand, he walked over to the large window where the faerie-fog swirled up against the glass. The fog retreated as though in response to his approach, then swirled back in, tendrils reaching out as though to touch him through the protective shield.

With his free hand, he raised his fingers to the glass, the stone of his ring—the sigil of the Legacy—clicking faintly against the cold surface. "Talk to me," he said softly, entreating. "You've proven you don't want to harm us, or release anything dangerous into this world. Tell me your side of the story. Tell us what we must do to resolve this peacefully."

But the mists were silent.

William Sloan was not a man who worried without cause. In his position within the Legacy, he was handed too many pieces of potentially bad news every day to take each one to heart. As his wife, Patricia, was fond of saying, there were only so many hours in each day, and so many days in each week. If he were to concern himself over every thing that went wrong anywhere within his knowledge, he would do nothing but sit on his rear and chew his nails until they bled.

So when the message come through to him that Derek Rayne had a problem at the San Francisco Legacy House, Sloan felt a twinge of concern about what his friend might be facing, and then stopped thinking about it. If Derek had felt that he needed help, he would have asked for it. Not willingly, no, but the other man was not a fool.

"Well," Sloan said, stopping to take a sip of his coffee

and grimacing when he realized that it had gotten cold. "Not too much of one, anyway."

Not enough that he would endanger the lives of his people over false pride. No, the fact that Derek was alerting others to a potential difficulty was just good procedure. Playing by the book. A rare concession from the stubborn Rayne and his equally stubborn and territorial crew, but nice to see. Maybe there was hope for them yet.

So it wasn't concern which made him pick up the phone late that night. No, he merely wanted to see how Derek was coming along with the codex he had been given to study, the one that was possibly involved in a monk's death. Had they made any progress or was it all a dead end? That was all. Nothing whatsoever to do with any possible problems that might be brewing.

"Of course, dear," Patty told him, patting him on the shoulder as she went off to bed. "What's important is that you believe that."

He smiled. All right. So maybe he was a tiny bit concerned. Only a bit. And only because he knew the trouble Derek's people could get into at the drop of a hat. As always, the question was not "was he paranoid," but "was he paranoid enough?" Derek had said that to him once, quoting that young hothead he had on staff, Nick Boyle.

In the years that he had known Derek Rayne, they had been at loggerheads more often than not. Derek carried a heavy burden on his back, the legacy—he winced at the pun—of his father's reputation, and history within the organization. And someday, perhaps soon, Derek was going to have to face up to the fact that he didn't need to carry that burden alone. But until then, all Sloan could do was be there. Whether or not the other man wanted his support.

The phone on the other end rang once, then clicked over to a recorded message that informed him that his phone call could not be completed. Putting down the receiver, a crease of worry formed between his brows. In and of itself, that was nothing. But . . . Are you paranoid enough?

Another call to the mainland assured him that there was no known difficulty with the phone lines in that area and that the weather had been clear, with only one small storm forming off the coast. Nothing that should have interferred with transmission.

He tapped a pencil against the paper-cluttered surface of his desk, frowning. Trouble reported at a House, and that House falls out of contact. Sometimes, it isn't paranoia at all.

Swivelling his chair, Sloan accessed his computer and tapped out a terse e-mail, asking about the codex. Nothing in the note referred to the problem Derek had indicated—nothing to suggest that this communcation was anything other than routine. That way, once this all blew over, Derek would have nothing to hold over his head and tease him about.

He finished the missive and hit the button which would send it on its way. The e-mail software flashed once, indicating that it had been sent successfully along the Legacy's intranet.

Yes, Derek was a big boy. He could handle whatever was brewing out there in San Francisco. Sloan would wait before upgrading this to active worry status.

Letting the monitor power down, Sloan pushed back from the desk and unfolded his too-lean length, stretching as he realized how late it had become.

"You're on your own, Derek. Try to keep your head above whatever water you're doubtless up to your neck in, hmmm?"

As he followed his wife's path to the bedroom, he

failed to see the screen power back up, and a message appear.

In small blinking letters, the display read: *message failure. system not active.*

ELEVEN

Rachel's head had barely touched the pillow sometime after two A.M. when the lights flickered on, gave off an odd sparking, sizzling sound, then snapped off again.

"What?"

Sitting up in bed, Rachel reached for the lamp beside her bed, then stopped, something telling her not to touch it. Then she felt a cold tingle pass along her shoulders, under her nightgown, as though a breeze had somehow entered her room.

The floor lamp across the room from her crackled on, then snapped off with an audible pop.

"Oh, wonderful." It wasn't bad enough that they were all running on next-to-no sleep without active phone lines, but now this? Reaching into her night table drawer, she pulled out a flashlight and snapped it on. The beam illuminated a narrow band, darting into the corners and shadows of her bedroom.

"Of all the times for a power failure," she grumbled,

then stopped. "Or maybe not." Having the power go out when the only weather aberration was caused by supernatural forces was a bit much of a coincidence. And she had always hated coincidences. Even before joining the Legacy. And especially afterwards.

Shrugging into her robe and belting it firmly, she opened the bedroom door and peered out into the darkness before venturing out. The familiar hallways of the Legacy House quickly became strangers in the flickering of her flashlight beam, her shadow dancing like a funhouse ghost. She shuffled down the hallway, trying to reassure herself that it was the same path she took every time she needed to use the bathroom.

"Right. Just me and my shadow . . . and a bunch of peevy elves doing a fandango on my nerves."

The wind still thumped against the exterior walls, echoing in the darkness and lending the sense of being trapped on the inside of a set of bongo drums. She shivered despite the fact that it was unseasonably warm inside the normally drafty building. *As though someone herded a flock of geese across my grave. Oh no, don't go there, Rachel.*

"Hey."

She yelped, jumped, then settled, her free hand pressed to her chest. "Hey, yourself," she said finally to Nick, who was leaning against the hallway wall, his own flashlight turned off. After seriously considering beating him over the head for scaring her, she played the light across his shoulders, careful not to hit his face for fear of damaging his night vision.

"Power out?" Rhetorical question, but she felt better covering all the possibilities.

Nick nodded.

"Not Mother Nature's fault," she guessed.

"Derek doesn't think so. All power to the island's been cut; electric, gas, even the water's down to a trickle. Computers are down. Even the emergency generator. Sucked dry. Very ugly."

"Wonderful."

"That about sums it up, yeah."

"What should we do?"

Nick shrugged. "Go back to bed? That's what Derek said he was going to do. Not a lot we can do, anyway, until the fog lightens a bit."

"You just going to stand there all the rest of the night like some buff gargoyle?" She smiled to take the sting from her words.

"Yep."

"In that case, I will go back to sleep. Have fun on guard duty."

Nick lazily tipped his fingers in salute, grinning. "Sleep the sleep of the just, m'lady, for your faithful knight is on the watch."

Her snort was his only reward for flippancy in the face of stress. Dropping the grin once she turned away, he listened to the soft slap-pad of Rachel's feet on the bare floor, trying to gauge the distance without looking, not wanting to rely on his eyesight alone under the current conditions.

When he heard her door open and close softly, he pushed himself away from the wall and started down in the other direction, planning to do a sweep of the upper floors, then downstairs, ending in the kitchen for a quick post-midnight snack. The ups and downs of the emotional roller coaster they were riding, topped off by his confrontation with Derek, had left him with a craving for something with an unhealthy amount of salt in it.

"Good thing I have such low blood pressure to begin with," he muttered to himself. "Because if I didn't, this place would kill me."

His flashlight hanging by his side, unlit, and a pair of night vision goggles tucked into his belt just in case,

Nick had just reached for the bannister when he felt the sudden rise of hairs prickling along the back of his neck. It was as though the familiar walls of the Legacy House had faded around him, dumping him in enemy territory.

"Oh, that's prime. Getting spooked by a little lights out?" he asked himself. "You're getting old. Pretty soon, you're going to need a walker—aigh!"

He jumped half a foot in the air, turning and landing in a defensive crouch.

"Sorry."

"Jesus." Standing, and making a note to apologize to Rachel in the morning, he shot Alex a glare that cut through the shadows. "Make some noise next time, okay?"

"I said I was sorry. What are you doing prowling the halls, anyway?"

"Just wanted to make sure everything was okay. You?"

"I . . ." She shuddered, hugging her shoulders. "I couldn't sleep."

"Bad dreams?"

"I'm not giving them the chance."

He nodded, understanding. "Come on. There's a bag of Doritos in the kitchen with our names on it."

"How do you manage to eat that stuff?" she wondered in disgust, but followed him down the hallway.

"Male metabolism. More proof that the male of the species is—"

"Don't start, Nick." Her tone was dry, the poke in the flesh of his shoulders sharp. "I am so not in the mood for your male chauvinist piglet squeals right now."

"So I guess asking you if it's that time of the month is out then, huh?" he joked, reaching up to turn on the light in the kitchen out of habit. She hit him again, right between the shoulder blades, and he staggered forward only half in jest, his hands coming up to protect himself from further blows.

"Okay, okay, truce, pax, no more . . ."

Smirking, she reached into the cabinets for the bag of Doritos she knew he had secreted there.

"Okay, time to find a new hiding place," he noted, pulling two sodas from the refrigerator and sitting down at the table.

"If you want to keep stuff secret," she said, sitting down opposite from him and dropping the bag on the table, "you're going to have to pick a hiding place that's not eye-level for everyone except you."

Nick considered her riposte, then made a mark in the air on her side of the table. "Point to her," he announced to an unseen audience. "Now gimme."

The ripping open of cellophane and the pop-open noise of cans were followed by determined munching. Seated in the dark room, with the only light coming from Nick's flashlight placed upright on the counter like a candle, a strange sort of peacefulness fell over them. More than coworkers, more even than friends, the silence was a comfortable one. And in that comfort, things that would have been difficult to say otherwise came naturally.

"David's trouble, Nick."

"I know."

"He's been lying to us all along."

"I know. But I can't just . . ."

She stopped to lick Dorito dust off her fingers, delicately, and washed it down with a swallow of Diet Coke. "I know."

TWELVE

D awn's eventual arrival was heralded by only a brightening of the fog that wrapped around the island. But the morning brought no answers, no blinding clarity for any of them.

Derek awoke from his uneasy slumber to discover that he had fallen asleep in the library, his head at an odd angle against soft upholstery. He had come down to take one last look at a book and . . . That was the last thing he remembered. Another victim of the infamous Comfy Chair. Alex would be amused. He rolled his neck experimentally, surprised when he could feel no cricks or soreness in the muscles there. If he could only remember what catalog he had ordered this chair from, he would order a dozen more. And one was going straight to Sloan. Maybe it would sweeten the cranky old man's mood a little the next time they clashed over something.

That thought was quickly pushed to the back of his mind as he came fully awake and the events of the previous forty-eight hours crowded to the forefront.

Standing and stretching to his full height, Derek acknowledged that, unless someone else had been given a sudden insight into their problem, all he had done was buy them a few more hours' time. Despite his comments about the relative lull the night before, he had no confidence that David's pursuers would hold off their attacks indefinitely. And if they did resume their attacks, it was unlikely that merely holding fast to David's leg and refusing to let go, as in the traditional tales, would dissuade their supernatural opponents to relinquish their claim.

"If only he had family, or someone who knew him, loved him here," Derek murmured to himself.

"I suppose that is why they cut us off from the mainland," a voice said behind him.

Derek turned abruptly, feeling a few more strands of his hair going gray. "Rachel. I didn't hear you come in."

"So I noticed. Did you spend all night here after shooing us all off to bed?"

His guilty, sidelong glance at the chair was all the answer she needed.

"Honestly, Derek, sometimes you're as bad as Nick."

"I suspect you are correct," he said, referring back to her first comment and completely ignoring her second observation. "Almost all faerie and folk tales have their basis in truth, and it is quite likely that a person with a sufficient emotional claim on David would be able to break the binding, whatever it is they have upon him."

"From what Alex was able to dig up, I don't think that there were many people left who cared that much about him," Rachel said regretfully, sitting down at the table and propping her chin up on one fist.

"That may be why he was playing us the way he did," Derek said, pacing the length of the table, his brilliant mind already churning over what they knew, trying to turn the fact of David Carson, human in need, into a more distanced logical problem. "If he could make us care about him to the extent that those emotional bonds were formed . . ."

"You think he was that calculating? Even hurt, the way he was?"

"I suspect that David Carson would have done whatever it took in order to secure his freedom."

"And could you blame him?" she asked softly.

He stopped then, facing her. "Blame him? No. I would not blame him. The drive, the sheer will to survive, is one of humanity's greatest gifts. But neither can I ignore the fact that he is not innocent in this matter and has by his actions endangered us as well."

"You were the one who said that the—God, it still feels weird to say it—the elves wouldn't hurt us."

"They have gone out of their way to avoid harming anyone so far," he corrected, sinking down in the staight-backed chair across the table from her. "A distinction with a difference, and one we need to keep in mind."

Alex chose that moment to walk into the library, a tall glass of orange juice clutched in her hands, and exhaustion rimming her eyes.

"Morning. We get struck with any brilliant ideas in our sleep?"

"Not unless you got one," Rachel said.

"Nope."

"Then we're depending on Nick to have a brainstorm."

"Don't hold your breath. I just left him, and about all he had on his mind was breakfast." Alex sat down at the long table, placing her glass down and scowling at the mugs already there, holding the dregs of the previous night's intake. "We've got to wash some dishes, and soon, or we're going to run out of mugs."

"Not to mention spoons," Rachel said dryly. "Someone's been eating their meals out of a peanut butter jar again."

Derek did his best "who me?" expression, then shrugged when she made a face at him. "We're out of bread, anyway," he said in mild self-defense.

Rachel shook her head. "If Kat starts walking around the house with a jar of peanut butter claiming that it's dinner, Derek Rayne, I'll have you up on charges of being a bad influence on a juvenile's eating habits."

"Getting back to the topic under discussion," he said quickly, "I suspect that such bonds would have to be deeper than we would be able to form over a few days' time."

"That's what you were hoping for, wasn't it? That Nick would be able to make that sort of a connection?"

Derek grimaced. "Among other reasons. But while David may desire such a bond in order to protect himself, I don't believe that he is capable of letting it form."

"He won't open up enough," Rachel guessed. "He's too scarred, too scared."

Alex turned her head, watching first one, then the other, catching up on their conversation that way.

"I suspect that he may not believe that he is worthy of such a bond, as well. Perhaps a remnant of what was done to him, more likely a result of whatever sent him onto the streets in the first place."

"What we have here," Alex said, having downed her orange juice and woken up a little more, "is a pretty basic conflict. David wants to be free of his hosts, for lack of a better word. And they don't want to let him go, whatever their logic. So, enter the Legacy into the equation. Playing devil's advocate here for a minute, we have an obligation to aid David, don't we? I mean, like Nick said last night, he's human, they're not. This should be what Kat likes to call a no-brainer." Years of debate class had left her very good at arguing a position she didn't believe in.

"Except of course for the fact that we have no idea how to protect him. All of our conjecture just now was merely supposition, based on myths and questionable documentation. None of which gives us anything solid to use in his defense. The one thing which might have worked—the truth of what was done to him—is denied us by David's own mental state. We cannot trust him simply on his word."

Rachel sank into a chair, stretching her long legs out in front of her and contemplating her sneaker-clad toes mournfully. "Add to that the time factor. They may not be willing to damage us, but we can't keep him here forever. For heaven's sake, we can't keep *us* here forever! As Derek said, supplies are already starting to run out. And sooner or later, someone's going to come looking for us. Are they going to be allowed onto the island? What will happen to humans who go into that fog?"

"So what do you suggest? Should we just hand him over, wash our hands and be done with it?" Alex sagged. "I'm sorry. I know you didn't mean that. It's just—I may not like him, Rachel, but I wouldn't send anyone back into the kind of existence he was describing. Nick and I have been talking it over all night. Morning. Whatever. Even if you write off some of it as his trying to manipulate us, the truth is, he was a slave, without even the most basic rights."

"Life, liberty, and the pursuit of happiness," Derek murmured. "But still . . ."

"What?" Rachel asked, hearing a change in his voice.

"Perhaps we have been looking at this the wrong way. Even you, Alex, despite your dislike for him, have been seeing David as a victim. An unwilling captive."

"Are you saying he's not?" Rachel's usually gentle voice rose a notch. "Oh, come on, Derek, you're not going to trot out that old 'he asked for it' line, are you? Because if you are, we're going to have to have a little sensitivity training session. With a clue × 4."

"The analogy is not an accurate one. Not entirely." Derek's voice warmed to the topic, speaking quickly, as though a pathway were opening up before him through crowded terrain even as his mouth formed the words. "But the fact remains that he made a deal, Rachel. No matter what we might think of those terms. And until we know for certain otherwise, we have to assume that he entered into it willingly, and of his own accord."

"He wasn't competent!" Rachel protested.

Derek nodded, hearing her argument if not completely buying into it. "No, I agree. Based on the physical and emotional state described in his medical records, he was not stable enough to make that sort of decision, even discounting the persuasiveness of faerie glamor. But that is a particularly human—no, an *American*—way of looking at it. We have a culture which makes a fetish of—" He noticed both women staring at him in various stages of amusement and distress, and put away the soapbox he had begun to climb onto. "Right. But that attitude is a recent development, and not one shared by the majority of the world's population. We need to look beyond those ways if we are to find a way to save him— and ourselves."

After Alex had left him in search of Derek and Rachel, Nick had spent a few minutes clearing up the remains of the snacks, wiping down the table with a handiwipe, and tossing the empty bag and cans into the trash. Once the gloom had risen a bit, with sunrise, he turned the flashlight off, thinking to save the batteries in case of a long-term blackout.

"Besides, I hate reading by candlelight, and odds are

good Derek's going to have us doing some more of that."

"Why don't you just ask me?"

Nick looked up to see David standing in front of him.

"Jesus, you move quiet," he said. "I didn't hear you come in."

"On little cat feet," David said, sitting down in the chair Alex had vacated. "That's me, the little man who wasn't there."

"You're mixing your poems," Nick replied. "And would you tell us anyway?"

"Huh?" David looked confused for a moment, then traced Nick's comment back to his own words. "Sure. Just ask."

Nick snorted, tossing the wipe into the sink and turned to face him, arms crossed over his chest. "You're going to tell me what's really going on in that head of yours?"

David looked up at him, his expression pure injured innocence.

"Cut the crap, okay?" Nick suggested, not unkindly. "You haven't told us anything that wasn't dragged out of you. And even then it was all spun deliberately, wasn't it? Saying what you wanted us to hear, painting everything the color you wanted it to be. You don't have to pull that game on me. I'm on your side. We all are." Then honesty forced him to add, "We might not be very happy with you, but we're the best allies you're going to find. And right now, it looks like we're your *only* allies." He paused for effect. "And you came looking for us, if you care to remember that."

David looked away, wincing at the emphasis Nick placed on his words. His hair, pulled back and tied at the nape of his neck, shone like a blackbird's wing in the limited light coming in through the kitchen windows, emphasizing the pallor of his skin. A careful observer could almost see the white of his bones protruding. "I . . . I don't know what you're talking about."

"Yes, you do."

Nick reached out, one hand almost touching the other man's shoulder before falling away. Alex was right. This stranger wasn't the innocent, the wounded child he so carefully played. He needed to remember that, to keep his distance, his objectivity. But the motion, and the gentleness of his voice, was enough to make David look up again; his expression was shuttered, protected, but his eyes held the faintest glimmer of hope, and Nick gave in, resigned to his karma.

"It's okay," Nick told him. "We'll get through this. Together." The anger he had felt toward David faded into dust. How could he stay distant? David might be manipulative, might be using them all—might be everything Alex suspected. But it wouldn't make any difference. Nick could no more turn away than he could cut off his own arm. It was partially a matter of honor—he had given his word. And partially, Derek had known what he was doing, throwing the two of them together. Nick was a sucker for someone in need of protection. And David was that, 110%.

"Do I have to deal with him again?"

Nick grinned despite himself, almost hearing the capital "H" in the other man's plaintive words. "Derek's not so bad. Don't worry, I'll protect you. Now let's get you some breakfast, or you'll have to protect me from Rachel. And trust me, she's scarier than Derek ever could be."

David managed a smile, and turned his attention to the pitcher of orange juice and tall glass Nick put on the table, slowly, carefully pouring himself some with a hand that shook under the weight of the pitcher.

Nick, busy pulling things out of the refrigerator, didn't notice. "Cheese, tomatoes, some bread . . . No power, so

188

I can't make an omelette. But I can probably whip up a pretty good icebox sandwich," he said, placing his supplies on the counter and sticking his head back into the open fridge. "Now, where's the mayo . . ."

"Oh no, David, that's too cruel, making you eat Nick's cooking."

Rachel breezed into the kitchen, casting a glance at the table where they sat before she reached into the cabinet for a glass and poured herself some orange juice from the pitcher. Her concerned gaze caught Nick's resigned one, and Nick nodded once, letting her know that he had everything under control for the moment.

Reassured, she went to the window and intentionally made a production of looking out into pearly gray swirls.

"So what's the weather update?"

"Heavy fog, with a 95 percent chance of elves," David quipped, then looked almost as surprised as Nick and Rachel at his words.

"A sense of humor emerges! Rachel, I think the patient may yet survive."

"Not if he has to keep eating your cooking, he won't," Derek said, coming in through the same entrance Rachel had used. The impact of the past two days could be read in the creases of his face and in the way his shoulders hunched forward just the slightest bit in exhaustion and worry. But still he held his face impassive, not allowing emotions to be read there.

The tension level in the room rose noticeably when the older man entered, but the three Legacy members pretended not to notice how David had gathered in on himself, like a child expecting to be beaten. Instead, Nick finished putting together a hefty sandwich and placed it on a plate in front of David.

"Don't listen to them. Eat. And what is this sudden running gag on my cooking? I've survived fine on it, thank you very much." He drew the weak joke out, as though it were a lifeline he could somehow tie around David's waist.

"Nick, you spend half your life taking women out to dinner, and the other half wheedling them into cooking dinner so you won't starve," Rachel retorted in the same tone of voice, for the same reason.

Derek, in the middle of pouring himself a glass of orange juice, quickly turned his laughter into a discreet cough when Nick mock-glared at him.

It was lighthearted banter worthy of an Emmy, considering the situation. The intended destination of this performance, however, seemed suddenly to lose track of the conversation, blinking rapidly several times and swaying. He placed the sandwich back down on the plate and opened his mouth as though to speak, but no words came out.

"David? Hey, pal, you okay?"

Before David could respond, or fall over—both of which seemed equally possible—Rachel was by his side, her fingers feeling for his pulse even as she scanned him for visible signs of trouble. A faint line of sweat sheened his hairline, and his breathing was a rasp in his throat.

"Get him upstairs. Now!"

Nick stood quickly, helping David to his feet and half-supporting, half-carrying him out of the kitchen. Rachel rose to her feet, her features creased in worry, and started to go after them. Derek caught at her arm, one thick eyebrow raised in inquiry.

"I don't know. It might just be the delayed reaction we talked about, the years he lost showing up all at once, full force. Or could they have, I don't know, done something to him? From out there, I mean." It was obvious from her expression that she hadn't considered that possibility before.

"Unlikely. If they could reach through the barriers to affect him directly, then why bother with such careful testing of our protections?" Derek shook his head. "No, I suspect that this has a much more obvious, physical cause. And so do you."

Rachel closed her eyes as though to deny what Derek was saying.

"You think that what he did to his body, the drugs and the damage, it's all coming back to him now?"

"Don't you?"

Her lips tightened, clearly unwilling to admit the possibility. "So all that time, free from drugs, and his body is only now reacting to the withdrawal symptoms? Derek, what you're suggesting is—"

"It makes sense, Rachel. If his age has been on hold for seven years, why not the rest of his body functions? Think about it. They offered him surcease from the pain, an end to the addiction. That would be the term of their agreement. And they have kept him alive, and healthy. But he fled from them, and their magic, and now, yes, I do believe that it is all coming home to roost, since his return to mortal lands."

"It makes sense," she admitted with a sigh. "I suppose I just didn't want to admit that there wasn't anything I could have done for him. I don't have anything here that would ease the symptoms, not without making the addiction worse in the long run, anyway. But if this continues, Derek, we're going to have more to worry about than physical deterioration. He may become emotionally unstable as well. Violent, perhaps."

"Will you be able to sedate him?"

"Adding drugs to his system, if we're right . . ." She let out a tiny huff of breath, clearly unhappy with her thoughts. "If it comes to that, yes," she said slowly. "If we have no other choice."

"Have a syringe ready," Derek instructed her. "Just in case."

• • •

Left alone when Rachel followed her patient out of the kitchen, Derek stared at the uneaten sandwich on the table and sighed. The mask slipped a little, and the sorrow showed in his eyes, outweighing the anger which had simmered untended all night.

"You run, and you run, but you cannot outrun your greatest enemy. And until you face it—yourself—you will never be free.

"Not even if you hide here forever."

Derek reached for the plate, intending to dump the remains in the garbage and put the dish into the sink, when his own words hit him. His face slid closed once again, and his gaze turned inward. Something tickled in his memory, the words he had read over and over again coming back to taunt him with something just out of reach.

"Hiding. Could it be that simple? Could it be . . ."

Leaving the dish untouched, he turned on his heel and headed back upstairs to his study. He needed to do a little more research. Those old books, with their conflicting information and wild suppositions, might just have the answer after all.

THIRTEEN

Left to her own devices, Alex sat in the Control Room and stared at the blank monitors, which had previously shown the tendrils of faerie intrusion into the house. Without power, they had no way of telling what was happening now. She took comfort from the fact that since their retraction after poking into the room where the chalices were kept, they had merely probed the contours of the security systems, feeling them out much the way a dog might sniff at a trail it wasn't overly interested in. They stayed far away from the rooms that stored artifacts of destructive intent, that same caution which had reassured Derek as to their non-aggressive intent toward the humans within. For the moment, anyway.

"They only want David," Alex whispered to herself. "Just David. We're not even secondary, just obstructions to be removed. But properly, like mining to avoid a cave-in. But why? Why is it so important to them to reclaim him? But not to the point of harming any of us, or—no, to the point of letting anything that we guard here loose. Major difference . . . but what do they care?"

Alex groaned, covering her face with both hands. *Well, that's the million-dollar question, now isn't it? Why all this, when it was pretty obvious they could force the Legacy's defenses down if they really wanted to? What in their damn faerie pride that folklorists loved to natter on about, what in their code the stories claimed no mortal could understand, was making them act this way, first aggressive, then careful?*

Trying to chase down all the threads and possibilities was giving her a headache the size and temperament of Godzilla. What should have been simple was becoming tangled, and she couldn't focus.

A thought occurred to her then, cutting through the fog of her brain and making her sit upright again. Their magical probes had not come near any human in the house, avoiding the areas which were heavily traveled. But if David could communicate with them—which it appeared he could—why couldn't she?

Going out to talk person-to-, well, fog, was out of the question; she wouldn't brave that stuff again if she had a choice in the matter. But she had other ways of butting her nose into other peoples' conversations.

"I really don't want to do this," she said out loud, but it was a token protest only. Now that she had thought of it, she wasn't going to be able to not try.

She had a brief thought that perhaps she should contact one of the others to keep her company, at least. *No. If I do that, Nick will protest, and Rachel will worry, and Derek . . . Besides, if I stop now, I won't have the nerve to do it again. Derek can yell at me later.*

Narrowing her eyes, Alex shut out everything else in the room; the uneasy silence of the computers, the scent and colors of the candles illuminating the room, even the ache of her own body as it protested sitting in one position for so long. And slowly her mind slid into the comfortable focus that often led to her clearest, most accurate psychic impressions.

Something cold. Severe. Shifting. Something very, very old. And not even remotely human. It was shifting restlessly, the sound of scales rubbing against each other; a dry, papery, itchy sound.

And then it Saw her.

ours.

No, Alex responded instinctively, lashing out against the possessive, seductive whisper. What David had described as beauty she saw only as an amorphous horror that made her back crawl with revulsion. Not-us, her every instinct cried out. Not friendly. Not mortal. Not welcome!

ours. The whisper was coaxing, but with an undercurrent of passion, the sense of sand slipping out through fingers, of a train racing headlong down a steep grade. An urgency that somehow translated itself from the voice to her sinews, making her quiver in body and spirit and want to give them whatever it was they needed, just to get them out of her brain.

"You have no right," she protested out loud, trying to slow down the flow of images and urgencies. She would not give in. She wouldn't! She couldn't.

sworn and bound. ours.

The whisper enticed her deeper, down and down into the swirling fog that had crept into her brain. No longer frightening but enticing. The flickering fascination of a bonfire made of ice, a sandstorm of glass. Faster, faster, it urged. Come to us now. Cold, sweet fingers stroked her spine, curling around her ribs and drawing her forward into the heavy alien nothingness . . .

"No!" she cried out, jolting to her feet in the empty room.

The silence echoed in her brain, leaving behind an emptiness she had never noticed before. An emptiness that had—even before her contact—been filled with fog. Drawing in a deep, shaking breath, she let it out slowly, and collapsed back into the chair.

"Oh boy."

"You spoke to them?"

Derek had come running, literally, in response to her instinctive mental shout of his name. One look at her face and he had gotten her out of the Control Room, out of that airless, stifling room. He seated her on the sofa in the library, where more natural light managed to creep through.

Forcing a glass of water into her hand, he watched like a hawk as she drank it slowly. Her hand still shook, but her color was better, and she could almost think about what had happened without going into a panicked mental tailspin.

"I don't know. . . . It wasn't so much talking as sensations. Like being immersed in an Impressionist painting, all shades and flowing colors. Nothing distinct, no definitions . . ."

Her voice trailed off, and she blinked, suddenly realizing how dry her eyes were from staring into nothing.

"You need to try again, see if you can contact them. Ask if we can come to some sort of agreement."

Alex shook her head, not taking offense at his insistence, knowing that only the dire situation could compel him to ask that of her. "Derek, I don't think they have the word "agreement" in their vocabulary. Or if they do, it means, 'you agree to do things our way.' "

"We don't have any other choice, Alex. If your theory is correct, they have been using a very subtle glamour to confuse us, to slow down our reactions. Now that we're aware of it, we should be fine. But I don't want to force them into violence if we can avoid it. Talk to them, try to work something out."

She finished the water, stared into the empty glass a moment, then looked up at Derek. "Why? Why now, all of a sudden? What happened to 'wait them out?' "

"Because now we know that we can communicate—"

"Derek. What's going on?"

He took the glass from her hand, where she had been twirling it idly between her fingers, and set it on the nearest table. "Something triggered my memory of something I had come across during our research. According to all the old myths, once you partake of their food, or accept their hospitality in other, specified ways, you must remain in their lands."

"Yes, so that's—"

"Let me finish, please. I've been doing some reading. Specifically, the work of one Sir Ellis Leithead. Somewhat of an eccentric, but he dedicated years of his life to the question of human and supernatural interaction. According to Leithead's research, if a mortal becomes entangled in the affairs of the fey, he might still recover his soul if he were to escape and elude them for a certain period of time."

"Like detox," Alex suggested.

"Yes, perhaps. I have never encountered that particular myth before, however, and so discounted it without supporting references. But then, while working on the question of supernatural influences and the memory, I came across something in a book I had not thought to research before, Topinka's *Mysteria*. Mostly, it deals with particular magics, the type of which have never concerned me, but I remember that there was something on the subject of souls caught up in supernatural events. Topinka seemed obsessed with that, in fact, especially on the subject of demons, but it does appear to support Leithead's theory.

According to this pamphlet, a human could free himself from a contract with a supernatural being if the human were able to remove himself from the demon's sphere of control. Topinka was speaking specifically of levels of hell, but—"

"But it does seem like that's what David is doing, doesn't it? All the delays, the hesitations and communications, all buying himself time, just in case we weren't going to believe him. Okay, so what's the time frame? How long do we have to hold out before he's free?"

"That is the problem. The *Mysteria* was far from precise on that. A failing all too common in the author's work, I am afraid. She was easily distracted by the next bright, shiny theory. And Leithead . . . well, obscure is a kind word for some of those passages."

"So, you want me to wriggle it out of . . . Them?"

"That would be a plan, yes."

Alex sighed, aware that he was right. If they had a definite goal, an ending point, maybe they could put together a plan to get there in one piece. She just didn't want to lower herself back into that snakepit if she didn't have to.

But, of course, she did.

And the voice had seemed pretty arrogant, so maybe it would let something slip if she poked it hard enough. But the thought of willingly going back into that seductive emptiness . . . It was alien, more alien than anything she could ever have imagined. Noone could have imagined anything like it, because the human brain just couldn't go there. And yet she was planning on intentionally walking down that path.

"I have got to be crazy," she muttered, too low for Derek to hear.

She shuddered, a cold prickle running between her shoulder blades, and suddenly found new sympathy for David. How could he have survived seven years of that and not lost his mind completely?

Maybe he hadn't.

"Okay. But you owe me for this, Derek."

"Dinner at the Garlic Rose?" he said, naming her favorite restaurant in the City.

"And a hot fudge sundae afterwards," she added, trying to lighten the atmosphere of the room a little.

"Deal."

Alex nodded, shaking off the sudden chill and trying to center herself. She wasn't going to be able to See anything if she was shaking like an aspen leaf.

One.

Her hands steadied, resting palms down on her denim-clad thighs.

Two.

Her breathing slowed, the thrumming of her pulse becoming a gentle hum.

Three.

Her eyelids sank closed, her face relaxing.

Four.

She tunneled inward, finding her center and grounding herself there.

Five.

She reached out, her own tendrils searching for that sweet, frightening vortex of fog and colors. And she found it, waiting just beyond her boundaries.

who?

Surprise. They had not expected her to come looking for them.

why? An aristocratic voice, formed of Alex's own expectations. She tried to See past it but was blocked. Whatever faerie held, it was not for her, apparently. She wasn't going to push it. She didn't want to save David that badly. Not if the cost was her own sanity.

We can work this out. Come to an agreement. Surely you can't spend forever waiting. She tried to inject as much persuasion and reasonableness into her mental voice as possible.

Laughter, mocking her mortal pretensions, flowed through her like a frozen knife, and her body shuddered violently. She could feel Derek beside her, holding her, trying to warm her body, but her attention remained focused on the swirling explosions of light within.

ours. sworn and bound. we wait.

And the vortex shoved her away, out and up and back into herself.

"Wow."

"I take it the response was not positive."

"Understatement. Derek, they have no intention of letting him get away. What's theirs is theirs, always and forever." She stopped, trying to find the words to fit what she had picked up from that brief, painful contact. "I think . . . I think the bargain he made with them, it's tied into their magic somehow. That's why they won't give up. If they did, it would weaken them. Maybe even . . . I don't know. But you were right, there's definitely something pushing them. Some kind of timetable. They said they would wait, but even in their arrogance there was a kind of desperation—very ugly. But also in a way kind of reassuring."

"Reassuring? How?"

"They're not invulnerable. They can be beaten. That makes them a little more understandable, less like monsters."

"No, not monsters. But amoral, all the legends and stories agree upon that. Do not let your guard down, even for a moment."

A tingling memory fought its way through the confusion, causing her to raise a hand to Derek's arm. "There was something else."

"What?"

"After they . . . kicked me offline, I guess, I felt something. Like . . ." She paused, trying to puzzle out the words to explain what she wanted to say. "What I Saw, heard, was their collective voice. But I think an individual tried to reach me as well. One of them speaking apart from the group."

"And? What did it say?"

Alex licked her dry lips, suddenly wishing for the glass of water again. "I think it was telling me that they won't harm us. Not even to get David. They don't want to hurt us. They just want what's theirs. But they're pretty close to immortal, Derek. Their minds don't work anywhere close to the way ours do. I don't know how to strip away the glamour, or even to sense if there's any still clouding my mind when I'm in there. Or even now. I don't know if we can trust them."

And together they turned to look out the window, at the thick, living fog swirling up against the glass.

●

FOURTEEN

The evening darkening of the mist brought with it an ominous silence. Apparently, with the humans inside all but ignoring their most recent actions, the faerie hosts outside had decided to cut back on some of their assault. The winds had been thumping and tapping at the exterior of the house so relentlessly for so many hours, that those inside had ceased to really hear it any more.

But once it was gone, the entire house sang with its absence.

More to the point, the total lack of the hum of electricity unnerved everyone more than they cared to acknowledge. Even Nick, able to rough it without qualm, admitted when pressed to missing the comforting glow of electric lights. Candles and flashlights just didn't cut it, long-term. Not within what should be civilization.

Derek stretched his legs out in front of him, leaning back into the embrace of the new chair—the "comfy" chair, as Alex had dubbed it, was living up to its reputation. But even the soothing feel of the forest green velvet upholstery failed to relax the muscles in his back and shoulders.

They had gathered in the library, flashlights abandoned for candles. Thick yellow votives sat on the long table, giving off a faint vanilla scent, while candelabras gathered hurriedly from display cases were scattered on smaller tables, their slender tapers burning steadily in the still air. It was barely eight P.M., but already they were exhausted. Of them all, only David and Derek had really gotten any sleep that night. Rachel had lain in her bed, staring at a ceiling she couldn't see, and wished for the late, late movie; Nick had paced the hallways, licking the crumbs of Doritos off his hands and waiting for something to jump out and go *boo!*; and Alex had retreated to a chair in her room, huddled in a blanket, trying not to let her mind relax.

They couldn't go on like this for much longer.

Knowingly or not, the fey had found the one thing that the members of the Legacy found almost impossible to combat: inactivity. Even more so than earlier, they were trapped with nowhere to go, nothing to do. Or so it appeared, at first.

The discovery that magic had somehow been influencing or muddying their thinking had been enough to break the spell, letting them shake off some of that torpor they only now recognized. But under the theory that a little prevention was worth endless if-onlies—and would give them something to do—Derek had sent Nick on a mission, with David tagging behind slowly, under orders not to stress his now-fragile body.

Armed with caulking guns and a paste laced with metallic glitter, the two young men were currently laying a careful pattern around the boundaries of the library and kitchen, and down the hallways connecting the two rooms, using David's intimate knowledge of their weaknesses. An occasional thump and low pitched laughter marked their progress, a hopeful sign that their relationship was slowly mending.

"If only we could get Nick to do that with as much enthusiasm for the weatherproofing," Rachel said from where she had collapsed into her own chair, studying her interlaced fingers with a little too much intensity.

"What are They up to?" Derek wondered, not really hearing Rachel's crack. "What are They waiting for?"

Alex came out of the open doorway to the Control Room, the usual holographic barrier down with the rest of the modern additions to the house. She looked even worse than the others, the lack of sleep and intense stress piling on top of her psychic exertion until she was practically drained. Her normally-glossy black hair was muted somehow, and her complexion was the color of ash in the flickering candlelight. She had been wandering through the rooms, a candle in hand, touching the inert machines with her free hand as though she could start them merely by sharing the electrical current natural to all humans. Nick, before escaping on caulk duty, had compared it to being at a multi-body wake, only without the booze.

"I wish you would try to get some sleep," Rachel said to her now.

"I can't. If I even start to fade off, I start hearing Them again." She shuddered, swaying a little and leaning against the nearest bookcase for support. "It's not—I don't want to risk it."

"You think they will try to harm you?" Derek said, getting up and motioning her into the chair.

"No. At least, I don't think so." She snuffed her candle between two fingers and sank into the upholstery thankfully, groaning a little as she did so. "Maybe. I don't know. I'm just so tired . . ."

"I think we have to assume the worst-case scenario

here," Derek said, picking up an argument that had been ranging all night. "As you said, we cannot trust them to hold to their assurances. If they were able to access your thoughts to any extent, they know that we have no intention of giving David up. Coupled with their assumed deadline, they have no reason to hold back any longer."

"So this," and Rachel made a lazy wave of her arms to indicate the entire house, "is just the lull before the big whammy?"

"So to speak, yes."

"Wonderful."

"You want me to try to contact them again?" Alex asked.

Derek looked at her, then shook his head. "No. Not yet, anyway. Just sit there and see if you can build yourself back up a little." He let out a sound of frustration mixed with exasperation. "If only I were able to follow the thread you see, to speak with them directly."

"Maybe they . . . David keeps referring to females much more than any male figure. Maybe they're all female? So it only works on the distaff side?" Rachel quirked one eyebrow at him, offering up a new side hypothesis.

"A possibility," he admitted. "There are some races of fey, elf-like, who appear only as females, but, if so, it's damned inconvenient."

Alex laughed, barely a shadow of sound. "Next time, we'll tell them to be P.C. about it."

"That would be appreciated." He touched her on the shoulder, briefly, and moved on across the room. Alex touched the spot where his fingers had rested, almost as though seeking reassurance from that touch of human warmth.

Rachel, watching this, frowned, thinking back over the past two days. Though they were all close in different ways, Derek wasn't much for touching. And yet he had been almost unusually demonstrative ever since the fog descended. As had Nick, now that she thought of it. Nothing overt, just a touch here or there, or standing a little closer than normal to other people—women—in the room. In another two men, in different situations, she would have called it flirting.

Here, though, under these conditions . . . she recalled something Derek had said, about emotional bonds keeping people, mortals, safe from fey influences. With ties to hold them here, a mundane link with which to dispel the fey glamour . . .

Like chimps, grooming each other not only to keep clean, but to reestablish the bonds of community. So that if one might be lost, it could still find its way home.

"They've been marking us," Rachel realized. "And I bet they didn't have a clue what they were doing." More proof, if they needed it, that the fey creatures were female. Even here, even as grounded as they were, the males of the Legacy were feeling the seduction.

But her amusement faded quickly. And the end result of giving in to that seduction was David; constantly coming downstairs when he should have been sleeping, his instinctive desire to survive craving contact, even when his injured soul clearly wanted nothing to do with them.

Derek thought it was too late to reach David that way, to create ties which would give him something to cling to against the riptide of elvish persuasion. But Rachel couldn't be so pessimistic. It wasn't in her, as a physician, as a mother, or as a member of the Legacy. And since Derek was to blame for that last fact, he was going to have to take the brunt of the fallout.

The clock in the dining room chimed ten times, its windup mechanism keeping it on-time despite the power outage. Using the cover of the sound, Nick pushed open a creaky first-floor window and stuck his head out. Dark mist swirled around him, and a few of the ever-present twinkly lights came over to investigate.

"Get out of here, you nosy tinkerbelles," he grumbled, swatting at them half-heartedly with one hand. "Can't a guy get some fresh air around here?"

Much to his surprise, they withdrew, leaving him alone. Alone. He had sent David back to his room to rest. Or the library, if he didn't want to be alone, saying that he was just going to take one last look around. Which he was. Only not in quite the way he might have implied.

He drew a deep breath, taking in the salt-damp air, crisped underneath with a hint of incoming autumn. But under these normal, familiar scents and tastes was the threat of something unpleasant, sour like sulfur or . . .

Brimstone.

"Don't get carried away. You're letting your feelings color your perceptions," Nick told himself, hearing Derek's voice in his words. "Don't project. Keep your mind open, clear; don't judge lest ye be judged . . . yadda yadda yadda . . ."

As he spoke, he pushed the window open to its widest, then lifted himself up onto the sill and, wiggling slightly, edged himself through the opening.

"Should've skipped dessert last weekend," he grunted. He was still pretty limber, but this was a stunt he would rather have left to Kat, all things considered. Using his upper body strength, he pulled free, dropping a few feet down to the concrete of the wide patio that ran along the side of the house. He winced at the impact, going into a ready crouch almost instinctively, wishing he had a gun with him while at the same time acknowledging the total uselessness of such an object in this situation.

But no lights returned to scold him, no quakes rumbled the foundation, nothing stepped out of the mists to confront him. So far, so good.

Straightening up, Nick dusted off his jeans and walked over to the low retaining wall of the patio. He had helped with the repairs to the wall just last summer, straining his arms and back to fit specially mined stones into place. His blood and sweat was in the mortar—he just hoped that it remembered.

"Let's see how good a job we did," he said, stalling for half a second. There was still time to go back, still time to not cross this particular Rubicon . . .

Placing his hands palm-down on the top of the wall, he vaulted over the foot-wide surface cleanly before he could allow any more second thoughts to creep in. This drop was much longer, but he landed squarely on shock-absorbing grass this time.

Still no outcry. He patted the side of the wall once in thanks, not feeling even remotely silly. After a while, you just stopped doubting that the house had it's own kind of aliveness. Even the extreme skepticism of Special Agent Dana Scully would've had to give in on that.

Well, maybe not. There was nothing that television writers couldn't find a way to justify. Unfortunately, life didn't work like that. No commercial breaks, either.

You're stalling again, a little voice said. This time, it sounded more like Phillip. One of these days, Nick was going to have a talk with the priest and former Legacy member about this unwanted conscience he had left behind.

Shoving his hands into the pockets of his light windbreaker—his usual leather jacket having been too thick to fit through the window with him—Nick strode off confidently, trusting his intimate knowledge of the island's landscaping to lead him to his destination.

Carefully not thinking about the small dock or the deep-sea kayak that was stored there, and shoving any idea of getting off the island out of his mind completely, Nick instead filled his mind with a not-entirely unforced enjoyment of getting out of the house, of being away from the people within. "Funny. I had forgotten how dark it can get out here, when you don't catch the lights from the mainland." Even the occasional candlelight flickering in the windows of the house behind him couldn't make inroads into the fog. But it wasn't unpleasant. More like being underwater, a different kind of world, but not one that was entirely unfamiliar.

After a moment, he began to whistle Frere Jacques, and the mist seemed to resonate with the cheery tune, refracting it back in swirls of lighter gray as he walked.

The ground underfoot changed from carefully-tended grass to rockier soil, indicating that he had left the grounds.

"Couldn't tell it from the scenery," he said to a swirl of gray that seemed to hover consistently just alongside and under his left ear, like an inquisitive hummingbird. Derek had speculated that the fog was a magical construct; not intelligent, but alive nonetheless. And so Nick treated it like one would a dog you weren't familiar with, speaking to it in a soothing voice, making no sudden moves, and at all times keeping his mind focused on going for a walk.

Based on the time he had been out, and the ground, he changed his path slightly, heading west. By now, he should have been able to hear the water clearly, but the fog muffled all sounds.

"If I suddenly get wet, I guess that's the ocean, huh?" The swirl didn't respond.

"Has anyone seen Nick?"

"He was here just a minute ago," Rachel replied, picking a book off the table and putting it on the reshelving cart for later. She was doing a remarkably good imper-

sonation of someone trying to look like she wasn't working just to keep busy, but Alex was too distracted to
notice.

"He said that he was going to do some more research,
but he's not here, and he's not with David—"

"Where is David?" Derek asked, leaning over the rail-
ing of the upper level of the library to join the conversation. He had a large, leather-bound book in one hand,
a flashlight in the other, and in the resulting shadows his
normally pleasing features flickered with satanic over-
tones. Alex shone her own flashlight upward in his direction and shook her head. "Taking another bath, if he
can get the water hot enough. It's a wonder we have any
water left in the pipes, the way he keeps washing."

"It's a normal reaction for someone recovering from
captivity," Rachel said, straightening a pile of papers and
pausing to read the top sheet. "He's trying to wash their
taint off his skin."

"He's not going to have any skin left, if he keeps that
up."

"Have you checked the kitchen?" Derek asked, dismissing the matter. "You know Nick firmly believes that
there is no crisis that cannot be headed off by application
of a good roast beef sandwich."

"Point taken," Alex said. "While I'm there, anyone
want anything?"

"What time is it?" Rachel asked, looking at her watch.
"Oh, for heaven's sake, it's almost ten o'clock! Derek,
have you had anything to eat this evening?"

An indistinguishable noise came from the upper gal-
ley.

"I'll take that as a no. Alex, if you do find Nick raid-
ing the fridge, just pile a tray and bring it back here,
would you? Best to congregate all of our available light.
I'll go let David know that he should join us as well."

• • •

210

Nick's knees were beginning to ache, and he had gotten tired of talking to the ever-present and uncommunicative fog. The tinkerbelle lights had left him alone, and he almost felt neglected. The ground under his feet was uneven, and he stumbled occasionally on rocks and torn up turf.

"Okay, this is not right," he said finally, admitting what he had known for almost half an hour. "There should be a shed, right about—there," and he waved in the general direction of what he thought was west, "and I should be on sand by now, not dirt."

With perfect timing, he stubbed his toe on something, and bit off an irritated curse. He hated to give in, hated to admit that he had been bested.

Except, of course, that he had.

"Okay. Okay, you win. I admit it. I'm lost in my own back yard. They're going to revoke my Scout badges, and put me on a leash. Can we go home now?"

There was pregnant pause, for a terrible instant he was afraid that they were going to make him grovel or something. And then the mist in front of him thinned slightly, as though being drawn away by some kind of air filter. Following where the path led, Nick found himself turning in a small half-circle. Then the air cleared completely, and he looked up.

"Well, I will be—"

He had figured that he was at least halfway to the coastline by now, a good mile from the house. But when the faerie fog let him get his bearings, it was by showing him the house, glimmering faintly with a kind of lambent glow, barely five hundred feet away.

He looked down, and saw that his feet were firmly planted on the lush, manicured lawn.

"You walked me in a full circle," he muttered, starting to get angry. "Leading me around like a bull with a ring through its nose. I suppose you found it all terribly amusing, didn't you?"

Not waiting for or expecting an answer, he stomped back up to the house, disdaining the way he had gotten out to instead climb up the long stone stairs up to the front porch. There was no point in trying to be a bad boy if everyone's already gotten your number.

Pushing open the front door, he was startled to see Alex crossing the entry foyer, looking just as startled to see him.

"Went for some fresh air," he said lamely, gesturing outside. As he did so, his watch sparkled in the light of her flashlight, and he stopped as though caught in ice.

"Nick?"

"What time is it?"

She frowned, holding the flash up to her own watch. "A couple minutes after ten," she said. "Why?"

He looked at his own watch, then lowered his arm. "Five minutes. I was out there for five minutes."

FIFTEEN

"Interesting move. Are you sure you want to do that?"

"Stop trying to psych me out, Derek. I'm about as messed-with, mentally, as I can handle right now."

"Sorry," the older man said, reaching forward to slide his own ebony chess piece across the board into the middle of a scattering of milky white ones. He sounded resoundingly unsorry. "In that case, check."

"Damn."

David, hanging over Nick's chair, let out a short burst of laughter, and Derek looked up to share an unexpected instant of camaraderie.

Rachel, curled up in a chair pulled next to the window with one of the many medical journals she never had time to keep up with open in her lap, looked up at that sound and caught the moment. Her argument might not have changed Derek's mind, but he had made an effort to include the newcomer in one of his and Nick's on-again, off-again chess tourneys. Notable more for sneaky invention than any classic moves, they involved good-natured abuse, accusations of cheating, and male bonding the sort of which stereotypically occurred only during sweaty team sports.

The picture the three of them made, the two seated over an elaborate chess table, the third leaning forward with the enthusiasm of a puppy, made her smile. Like soldiers knowing the final battle was near, they seemed to have put aside all differences, all arguments, to conserve their strength for the coming battle. But if you ignored that fact, the dire shadows it painted around them, it was a charming picture. She turned her head, meaning to call Alex's attention to the scenario, and her smile froze, then faded.

"Derek!"

Her urgent whisper carried across the room, and caused the prefect to look up from the endgame he had created. She jerked her head in Alex's direction, and Derek followed with his gaze, then stood up abruptly, pushing his chair back so quickly it fell over.

"Alex?"

The young woman didn't seem to hear. Her brown eyes were shaded with the fog which still swirled outside, her lower lip clenched between her teeth hard enough to draw blood.

"Alex?" Nick got out of his chair and started forward, but Derek put a hand out to stop him. "No, wait."

"What's wrong with her?" he demanded.

"They're talking to her," David said. He hung back, his momentary lapse into humor fading into white-knuckled fear. "They're here." His voice was petulant, a little boy's terror expressed badly.

"They've been here for days," Derek snapped. "Shut up and sit down, David."

David sat down in the chair Nick had vacated and

picked up one of the black quartz chess pieces, rolling it nervously in his hands. His gaze shifted from Nick to Alex to Rachel, carefully avoiding Derek. All the emotional progress they had made in that afternoon had vanished, but Rachel couldn't take the time to mourn it now.

"Alex? Can you hear me, Alex?"

"I can . . . I can hear you."

But it wasn't her voice.

David yelped, jumping up and backwards, so that the chair fell to the ground behind him.

"It's Her. It's Her, oh God make her go away I don't want to hear her I don't want to see her, I can't stand it make her go away . . ."

"Nick!" Derek yelled. "Get him out of here."

Nick pulled on David's arm, leading him from the room. He moved like a sleepwalker, stiff-limbed and shaking, moaning under his breath.

"Rachel?"

"No," she said, responding to Derek's unspoken suggestion. "Alex needs me more. Nick can handle it."

Alex raised her head then, her fog-grayed eyes glowing with tiny sparks of indescribable color. The same color which swam through the fog outside.

"You will give us the sworn one."

The voice was sweet, reasonable, honey and lime curling into their ears and coaxing their hearts.

"You will give us the sworn one. He is ours. He will go with us and all will be as before."

"I cannot allow that," Derek said firmly.

"Why not?" The voice sounded genuinely curious.

"He is a human being, with rights."

"He is sworn. He is ours. We . . ." The voice seemed to be searching Alex's brain for the right words. "We maintain what is ours. There has been no . . . No breach. No failure of the swearing on our side."

"You swore to take care of him." Rachel said, accusingly, refusing to step back when the creature using Alex turned that inhuman stare onto her.

"Yes."

"And you call what he has been through 'care'?"

"He is well. Fed. Healthy. He lives young forever. His needs are met. All as we promised. He is sworn. He is ours."

"He does not belong to anyone!" Derek protested, his voice rising in anger. "I defy you, and I defy your claims. You may not have this mortal soul to be your play toy!"

The wind hit the windows all at once, in a renewed blast which made the state-of-the-art frames rattle like old leading. Rachel's face blanched, but she didn't move from her position. Derek seemed unmoved, a figure made of granite.

"If you're going to attack, get it over with," he said to the room at large. "Enough with the talking! Take him, or leave us be!"

The wind died down, leaving a stillness that was more deafening than any explosion could be. "You can't, can you?" Derek said. "You can't attack us directly. Not physically. You can threaten, and cajole, and harry us until we give up of our own free will, but physical violence is out."

He turned to Rachel then, slipping for just an instant from warrior to researcher. "Alex must have been opening her mind to them, inviting them in to talk to us, and they took her up on the invitation. Free will is the key. They can use their magic to cajole, to seduce, but not to force. If we can just stand firm, their time will run out and they will be forced to concede him to us."

At his words, Alex's body shook like a marionette with tangled strings. Her mouth opened, teeth clicked, and a new voice came through. It was a heavy echo, the complex blending of a screech owl's hoot, the whisper of earthworms, the scream of a mouse caught in talons, the cold shudder of the night wind. And it cut through the warm familiar comfort of the library like a serrated blade.

"Why do you interfere? By what right do you interfere? Does he belong to you? Has he sworn to you as well?"

"No," Derek was forced to admit. "He has not. But he has asked us for aid and protection. To us, to those within this building, that is a tie as binding as any sworn oath."

The voice speaking within Alex hesitated, again searching for the right word.

"Tough."

And Alex collapsed onto the floor, her strings cut, her limbs abandoned by her puppet masters. Rachel raced forward, raising her back into her chair and fussing over her as Alex slowly came back to herself.

"You okay?"

"Yeah. Yeah, I think so. Wow, talk about your Mack trucks . . ."

While Alex babbled, Derek turned on his heel and walked over to the nearest window. Raising one hand to the glass, he placed his palm against the cold surface and pressed it flat. The fog touched at him, through the glass, and backed off a pace, like a cat stepping into cold water.

"I know you now," he said to it. "I know what you want."

"Derek?" Rachel was calling him, asking for his help with the exhausted psychic.

But he did not respond, staring into the depths of the fog.

There are days when I wake up and know exactly what I believe, what I think, and what I intend to do. But since the faerie fog descended upon us—since David came to reside within these walls—that has not been the case. And the spell which clouded our minds cannot take all the blame.

For the Voice, both Voices, while speaking selfishly, merely made audible what has been in the undercurrents of my mind all along. What right have we to interfere with a contract, duly agreed upon and executed, and then broken by one side without cause? David swore his fealty, and we have no claim to interfere, not of kinship nor affection of blood or heart.

Rachel and Nick would disagree, saying that the fact that he is human alone gives us that Right. That he was coerced, and so cannot be held against his will.

But I am not so certain.

This is not so clear cut a case as we have faced before. Amoral the fey who claims him may be, and cruel, as we judge these things. But that was not the sound of callous indifference I heard in the first voice. Nor was it a voice of evil, of the Darkness.

We call these beings faeries, or elves, and ascribe to them what we think we know of such beings. But all we know is merely what our eyes can see, and our brains conceive. And the reality may be something far more encompassing than the outlines we construct to hold them.

Whatever they are, I know that they will not harm him, that they are, perhaps, his only hope. And so, what should we do—maintain him here, and risk what fallout might come of that? Or do we return him to those who are best suited to protect him, even if that protection is only from himself?

This is a decision no one should ever be forced to face, a power no one should ever hold over another. And yet, the decision must be made. And made soon, or it will all become moot.

And David deserves more than to allow inertia and indecision to decide his fate.

SIXTEEN

T he silence and growing darkness both inside and out
    eventually forced them all back to the library, which
seemed the only room immune to the escalating ten-
sions. Rachel had brought her diary down, and was making careful entries by the light of a thick candle. David
and Nick had taken over the chess game, barely speaking
as they pondered dead-end moves. David's shoulders
were wracked occasionally by violent coughs, and even
in the warmth of an afghan thrown over his lap he shivered. Alex, curled in the comfy chair as though it were
her mother's hug, stared at Derek.

And Derek, his back to them all, seemed a statue.
Unmoving, barely breathing, he seemed not to have
moved from his position since Alex's channeling of the
faerie presence.

Finally, Alex couldn't stand it any more. Ignoring David's presence in the room, she burst out, "What are we
going to do?"

Everything stopped. David visibly shrank in on himself, then looked to Nick for support. But Nick was looking at Derek as well. His face was tightly drawn, as though holding back protests, but his body language was that of a soldier awaiting orders. Orders that he realizes will be unpleasant.

"There comes a time when certain truths must be faced," Derek said finally, his voice muffled by the fact that he was speaking toward the window. "And the truth here is that we—I—cannot, in conscience, use force to keep David from his fate."

"But—"

"Derek, you can't—"

"No!"

It was David's voice, trailing off into painful coughing, which silenced their outbursts.

"You promised! You promised to protect me!"

"Protect you from what?" Derek asked, finally turning to face the younger man. "From an agreement which you entered into freely? Without coercion?"

"They lied to me!"

"You made assumptions," Derek retaliated, forcing himself to remain coldly distant. That was the only way he was going to get through this. "And you have suffered for those assumptions, I will not deny it. But that does not give us the right to interfere in a legitimate bargain."

"I'll die there," David threatened.

"You'll die here faster."

Those words fell into a room silenced by the certainty in Derek's voice. He looked up at Rachel, who nodded.

"He's right, David. You know he is." She went to his side, resting one slender hand on the top of his head in a soft, maternal caress. Her white skin shone against the dark brown of his hair. "We've all seen the signs. Whatever they did to fix you seven years ago, it's falling apart now. The damage you did was too much, your body can't repair itself. Not by any means known to our medicine, anyway."

"If he was willing to go into rehab," Nick ventured, "would that . . ." His voice trailed off when he saw Rachel shake her head.

"It is too late. So long as he remains in this world, in the mortal realm," Derek said, "he will continue to suffer the consequences of the damage he did to himself." He turned to the young man, speaking directly to him, with all the sincerity and persuasion he could muster. "You are right. We did promise to protect you, to keep you from harm. But allowing you to stay here would run counter to that promise. Your only chance of survival is to return with them. Let them restore you to health."

"No! I won't go back there!"

"They've cared for you, in their own way," Rachel said in a coaxing voice, still stroking his hair. "They're worried about you."

"I don't care," David sulked, turning away. "I'd rather die than go back there."

The Proctor of the Legacy sighed, regret thick in his voice. "Then that is your right. But we will not aid you in your suicide."

Nick opened his mouth to protest, then subsided, sitting down heavily and staring at nothing in particular. He didn't like what Derek was saying, but he had nothing to argue with that hadn't already been said. And one look at David's face showed that Rachel was right. In three days, he had become obviously weaker, his flesh shriveling off his frame. A nervous energy animated him now, and his eyes couldn't stay fixed on one object but instead constantly flitted from one person to another.

David snorted, a dry, unpleasant sound. "What are you going to do, hand me over to them?"

"No," Derek said. "But we will not raise force against

them, either." He ran a hand through his hair, looking for the right words to say. "This is your life, David. It's a precious gift, one you have been given a second chance with. You have a choice to make: either honor your word to the ones who took you in, and live, or—"

"Or be thrown to the Hunt?"

"Or take your chances against those you have broken faith with. We will feed you, clothe you, give you the medical attention you will soon need, but no more."

David stared at him, then looked to Nick, Rachel, and Alex in turn. Rachel met his eyes, but the other two looked away. They might argue with Derek, but in this, matters regarding the safety of the Legacy, his word was Law.

"The hell with you, then. The hell with all of you." David bit the words off, snarling, his eyes wild and not entirely sane. "I'd rather take my chances with the Hunt than humans like you."

"Sleep on your decision," Derek said, refusing to be baited. "We'll discuss it in the morning."

"Things might look better once you're rested," Rachel said, trying to inject hope into her voice but failing noticeably.

David raked them all with a scornful glance, then got up and walked out of the library. His gait was unsteady, but his back was straight, and he didn't look back.

"David!" Nick called, getting up to follow, but Alex stopped him with a hand on his shoulder. "Leave him, Nick. You can't do anything for him now."

"If he runs, it will kill him, just getting off this island." Rachel said quietly to Derek. "And he doesn't care. He'd rather die than live with them. What kind of choice is that?"

Derek gave no answer.

• • •

For the third night in a row, the inhabitants of the Legacy House tried to get some sleep. And, for the third night in a row, they failed. But this time, it was not the uncertainty of siege mentality that left them wakeful, but the oppression of decisions made and consciences weighed.

And the weight was heavy.

Derek looked up without surprise as Rachel entered the library, bearing a lit taper that cut through the gloom he had been sitting in. She had put on a nightgown and robe, and her hair showed the tousled results of having touched down on a pillow, but her eyes were clear and her face was lined with exhaustion.

"You're the last one," he noted. Her eyebrows raised in question. "Alex wandered through here half an hour ago, looking for something to read."

"And Nick?"

Derek sighed. "The last I heard from him, he was single-handedly decimating the contents of the refrigerator. Apparently, he was concerned about the effects of the power outage on . . . well, everything, based on the height of the sandwich he was building."

Rachel winced. "The appetite of a growing boy."

"I'm afraid that the only thing growing on him right now is his anger."

"At you?"

Derek nodded. "And at himself, as well. He gave David unquestioned support, a camaraderie of sort, and now he has been forced by my decision to throw that back in David's face. And the fact that he did not contradict that decision. It is difficult for him."

"It's difficult for all of us. You especially. Don't try to pretend that this was any easier for you than anyone else."

He shrugged, going back to staring into the shadow-shrouded bookcases.

"And David's own actions had a great deal to do with our decision as well," she reminded him acerbically. "Don't get so wrapped up in your own responsibility and let him escape a share of the blame."

His only response was a low snort. Placing the taper on the nearest clear surface away from the books, she walked over to stand over his chair, her hands reaching down to touch his shoulders in a comforting gesture. His hands lifted to cover hers, and they stayed that way for a moment.

"I wish . . ." Her faint Southern accent returned in full force with those two small words.

"Yes. So do I. But no matter how I rethink it, no matter how many different routes I trace, different decisions I make, it all comes out the same way. We had no right to interfere, and so by the rules of the magic which bound him, we *could* not interfere."

"Nick knows that."

"But what he knows, and what he feels, are not always in sync. And that is what is angering him."

"Now, who's the psychologist here?" she scolded, squeezing his shoulders once to indicate that she was teasing. "If he knows this, and you know this, you'll manage to get back to normal sooner rather than later. That's what family does."

"Family. Yes." Derek would have said more, but as he raised his head to look up at Rachel, the scene out of the Library's main window caught his attention.

"Rachel!"

His urgent whisper drew her gaze to what he was looking at, and her hands fell away as she took a step forward, toward the window.

The window where the faerie fog was beginning to change. Even in the darkness of night it was obvious. The mists thinned, then contracted, writhing as though undergoing some violent internal convulsions.

"Derek . . ."

"I don't know," he said, shaking his head.

Even as they watched, the fog drew in on itself once again, thickening into ropes of sparkling lights twirled within the darkening gray mass. And then the ropes twined around the house like a lazy cobra wakening, and were gone.

"Oh, God . . ."

"David."

Derek shot to his feet, running for the stairs, Rachel close behind. But they knew what they would find, even before they ascended the stairs to the guest wing.

Sure enough, the bedroom was empty, the bed denuded of sheets. The window casement was pushed open, the edge of one sheet tied securely to the winch.

"He couldn't wait until the morning," Rachel said, coming out of the bathroom. "From the looks of it, he showered, changed into fresh clothing I had left for him, including a pair of Nick's old running shoes, and left."

"He didn't want to use the door. Why?" Derek wondered, going to the window and touching the sheets forming a makeshift ladder.

"He knew we were downstairs. He didn't want to face us."

"That doesn't make sense. If he had wanted to, there were exits out of the house much easier than this, and we wouldn't have known he was gone until—"

"But they would have." Alex arrived in the doorway, with Nick half a step behind her. "We saw the fog lift from the kitchen, guess we figured it out the same as you."

"You think he did this, climbed out the window, in order to catch the elves off-guard?"

"This room was still doubly warded. So it would have been like a blank spot on their radar, or whatever. Maybe it extended a little past the window, giving him some extra time."

"They must have known that he was ill," Rachel agreed. "They were probably hoping he would just walk out the front door, and they'd have him."

"Nice to know that they're not all-powerful," Nick said, finally coming into the room and going to stand by the window alongside Derek. "Maybe even a little lazy, waiting for their prey to come to them. That way they didn't have to do any work, like securing possible escape routes." There was bitterness in his tone, but he wasn't lashing out, and Derek took hope from that. The younger man reached down, and began to haul up the sheets.

"Do you think . . . do you think he got away?" Rachel wondered, rubbing the sides of her arms as though cold.

Nick pulled the last of the sheets in and gauged the length in his hands.

"Well, he hit the ground running, that's for sure. This was long enough to get him down three stories, just a short drop to the patio, and then over the balcony. For someone in good health, not a problem." He let the obvious remain unspoken. "Odds are, we won't ever know if he makes it or not. Unless one of the fey decides to come back and fill us in."

"I'd be just as glad if we never have to deal with them ever again," Alex said fervently.

Nick nodded, his mouth set in a grim line, and dropped the knotted sheets in a pile on the floor. "I guess we should be getting power back soon. I'll go check on the fuses and see what's up with that."

Derek nodded, leaning forward to start rolling the windows closed. "Yes. With David no longer within these walls, they would have no reason to—"

The window was halfway closed when a faint, inhuman wail rose from the direction of the beachfront facing the city. It was the grieving noise of an animal, a keening scream of denial.

And then all was silent.

The room was frozen, even their heartbeats stilled in the moment. Time stretched into an eternity, painful and numb all at once. An owl called, its low hoot a mournful coda to David's final mortal sound.

EPILOGUE

"He would have had a better chance had he waited until morning."

Derek stood by the window, his gaze fixed. Dawn was beginning to touch the sky in dark pink streaks, while in the near distance, the lights of San Francisco still flickered underneath. After so long encased in gray, the clear colors seemed almost obscene. Obscene that life went on.

"Stop that."

He startled, having forgotten that Alex was in the room with him.

"I was just—"

"You were just thinking that it was unfair, that we were going on with our lives," and she indicated the scene outside with her hand, "that they are going on with their lives, and David is trapped in a place far from home."

"Yes." His wide mouth stretched into a self-mocking

smile without humor. "I suppose that I was."

"We spend so much time fighting for others, keeping them safe without their ever knowing . . . sometimes I think that we forget we can't solve every problem, protect every person."

"It's our job. To protect. To stand between the darkness and the light."

"Sometimes it's an impossible job." She paused, raising her hand to touch him, then letting her hand fall away without contact. "And sometimes just because something is shadowed doesn't make it dark. Think, Derek. Even if we had been able to win him away somehow, how long do you think he would have lived? With the damage returning to his body, the addiction still in him? What kind of life would it have been, always longing for faeryland, even hating it the way he did? No, it's better this way. They'll take care of him."

"A prisoner."

"Alive."

"Did you ever see the *Star Trek* episode 'Charlie X'?"

"No," Alex shook her head, even though she had, in fact, and knew exactly what point he was going to make.

"They rescue a young boy, raised by aliens. But he's been changed by his stay. And they have to let the aliens take him away again, for his own good."

"See? Even Kirk couldn't save everyone," she joked.

He smiled, but only briefly. "But David wasn't a child, was he?"

"Worse. He was an adult, who made his own decisions and then had to face the consequences." She did touch him then, a gentle brush of her palm across his arm. "Let it go, Derek. You can save the world, but you can't always save everyone in it."

Her point made, she left him there, staring out across the water at the strands of fog visible in the rising dawn as they curled around the outskirts of the city.

• • •

Alex was correct. Much as we struggle daily against the forces of darkness, there will always be battles we cannot win. And so it was with David Carson. He had made a deal that did not end as he had expected, no, but that is the risk when dealing with the unknown. No doubt he curses our names, wherever he is now. But he is alive. And, in time, I believe that, like the humans of legend taken in by the fey, he will grow to prefer his new home. Or at least feel welcome there.

We acted cruelly, I do not deny that. But the truth is that cruelty is often a kindness, and kindness a terrible cruelty. And the line between the two is often merely the width of interpretation.